"Come on, you must have *some* fond memories."

"Not really. The tree went up a few days before Christmas, came down the day after. Presents were opened Christmas morning."

Watching him, Rae couldn't help but feel as though she was missing something. He looked so sad.

She couldn't imagine not having *some* happy memories of Christmases past. Only part of the reason she was determined to make things special for Maggie and Max.

"Mr. Cole!"

He looked in Max's direction. "What's up, buddy?"

"Wanna come help me slide?"

"Are you kidding?" Cole's countenance brightened as he pushed to his feet. "I live to help you." He winked at Rae. "Duty calls."

She shook her head as he walked away. Maggie and Max weren't Cole's duty. Yet he had embraced them. Gone out of his way to make sure Max didn't see him as a threat. But the sorrow she'd seen when he spoke about his Christmases tugged at her heart and made her want to include him in her holiday plans. To prove to him that Christmas really was the most wonderful time of the year.

Award-winning author **Mindy Obenhaus** lives on a ranch in Texas with her husband, two sassy pups, and countless cattle and deer. She's passionate about touching readers with biblical truths in an entertaining, and sometimes adventurous, manner. When she's not writing, you'll usually find her in the kitchen, spending time with family or roaming the ranch. She'd love to connect with you via her website, mindyobenhaus.com.

Books by Mindy Obenhaus

Love Inspired

Bliss, Texas

A Father's Promise
A Brother's Promise
A Future to Fight For
Their Yuletide Healing

Rocky Mountain Heroes

Their Ranch Reunion
The Deputy's Holiday Family
Her Colorado Cowboy
Reunited in the Rockies
Her Rocky Mountain Hope

The Doctor's Family Reunion
Rescuing the Texan's Heart
A Father's Second Chance
Falling for the Hometown Hero

Visit the Author Profile page at LoveInspired.com.

Their Yuletide Healing

Mindy Obenhaus

LOVE INSPIRED

INSPIRATIONAL ROMANCE

LOVE INSPIRED®
INSPIRATIONAL ROMANCE

PLEASE RECYCLE
THIS PRODUCT IS RECYCLABLE

Recycling programs
for this product may
not exist in your area.

ISBN-13: 978-1-335-56739-0

Their Yuletide Healing

Copyright © 2021 by Melinda Obenhaus

This edition published by arrangement with Harlequin Books S.A.

For questions and comments about the quality of this book, please contact us at CustomerService@Harlequin.com.

Love Inspired
22 Adelaide St. West, 40th Floor
Toronto, Ontario M5H 4E3, Canada
www.LoveInspired.com

Printed in U.S.A.

I am come that they might have life,
and that they might have it more abundantly.
—*John* 10:10

For Your glory, Lord.

Acknowledgments

Stories are never possible without a little help along the way. Many thanks to Engineer Operator Kevin Courtney and Terri Brasher, RN, for helping me bring Cole and Rae's story to life.

Chapter One

Just when Rae Girard thought her life in the small town of Bliss, Texas, had become truly blissful, Tilly Becker walked into Rae's Fresh Start Café and burst her bubble.

The aroma of coffee and bacon still hung in the air Thursday morning as Rae watched the last two ranchers, part of a group that gathered for coffee every morning, wave on their way out the door, leaving her with the spry seventy-eight-year-old with a spiked white pixie cut and sassy, blue-rimmed glasses.

"'Bye, fellas." Grateful they were alone, except for her cook and a couple of waitresses, Rae jerked her gaze back to Tilly. "What do you mean *I'm* in charge of the Mistletoe Ball?"

Tilly had been coordinating the event scheduled to take place just a little over a month from now since its inception a decade ago. The Mistletoe Ball was an elegant evening of dinner, dancing and donating. The silent and live auctions that benefitted Bliss Children's Ranch and foster families were always the highlight of the night, if not the entire holiday season.

Invitations had already gone out for this year's gala, ads had been placed in the local newspaper, signs were all over town. And this year, the Mistletoe Ball was being held at the newly renovated Renwick Castle, which would, no doubt, boost attendance. And yet Tilly wanted to put Rae in charge?

"I suppose I should have explained myself first." The older woman toyed with one dangling earring.

"Ya think?" Rae sucked in a breath and willed herself to calm down. Perhaps she'd misunderstood Tilly.

"Let's wait until Cole gets here, though." Tilly looked at her coyly. "You remember my nephew, don't you?"

"I know who he is, yes." Local attorney. *Very* handsome. Partial to nicely tailored suits, the way Rae's ex-husband had been. Unlike her car salesman ex, though, Cole wasn't the most personable fellow. Friendly, yes, but he always had a sad air about him. His smile never quite reached his eyes. "Why is he coming here?"

"I'll explain once he arrives."

Rae checked her watch, noting it was a little after ten. Cole had better hurry. Folks started rolling in at eleven for lunch.

Following Tilly's gaze to one of the large windows that flanked the entrance, she noted the cornstalks, pumpkins and colorful mums alongside the metal benches perched beneath the ancient live oak and magnolia trees around the courthouse across the street. Soon they'd be gone and a large Christmas tree would adorn the square, along with a massive red-and-white sleigh that was perfect for photo ops.

"Here he is now." Tilly scurried toward the entrance in her flowing leopard-print tunic and black leggings and swung open the door. "Thank you for coming on such short notice, Cole. I know you're a busy man."

And Rae wasn't busy? She was the sole proprietor of the most popular breakfast, brunch, lunch and specialty coffee place in Bliss, as well as a foster mom. Since coming to live with her this past May, six-year-old Maggie and five-year-old Max had brightened her world with their sweet smiles and crazy antics. Not to mention school projects, church activities, trips to the park to expend energy and more laundry than she'd ever imagined possible. Now she could hardly wait to give them a Christmas they'd never forget. One with all the twinkling lights, festive decorations and holiday happenings folks enjoyed in those Christmas movies she'd already begun watching. After all those kids had endured in their short lives, they deserved something special. Rae would do anything to see them happy.

Tilly closed the vintage wood-and-glass door before escorting her nephew across the worn wooden floorboards. "You know Rae, don't you, Cole?"

His tie was missing today, but that pale blue button-down with the light navy suit sure highlighted his silver-gray eyes. Eyes that failed to hold even the slightest hint of a spark.

The man with neatly trimmed brown hair slipped a hand from his pocket and extended it toward Rae. "Good to see you again." As if they ever really saw each other. He wasn't a frequent customer, though he'd occasionally pick up a lunch special or dine with a client.

She wiped her hand on her black half apron before reciprocating. "You, too."

"I'm going to cut right to the chase." Tilly pressed her hands together and linked her fingers. "My daughter, Shelly, has broken her back."

"Oh." In the blink of an eye, Rae went from annoyed to humbled. "That's terrible."

"I'm sorry to hear that." Cole's voice remained calm.

"I'm headed up to Waco to help her and her family while she recovers." She eyed Rae. "Shelly and Dwight have a twelve-, fourteen- and fifteen-year-old who are all active in sports and what have you. And, given that Dwight has to travel for work, I need to be there to help keep things running as smoothly as possible."

"How long will you be gone?" Cole's brow furrowed.

"Shelly won't be able to drive for at least six weeks."

"*Six weeks?*" Eyes wide, Rae simply stared at her friend.

The woman nodded. "The two of you know better than anyone how passionate I am about the Mistletoe Ball. It is my baby, after all."

Rae felt the pressure mounting, constricting her throat.

Lifting her chin, Tilly continued. "You're also aware that I do *not* like to ask for help unless it's absolutely necessary. This is, sadly, one of those times. Rae, you're already second in command for the Mistletoe Ball, so you'll be filling my shoes."

"Tilly, I—" No one could possibly fill Tilly's shoes. She was the one with all the knowledge and experience, not Rae. "This is only my second year as co-coordinator. There's no way I'll be able to handle everything by myself." Besides, last year her time had been her own. Now she had two children to care for.

"I don't expect you to. That's why I asked Cole to join us." Her dark gaze shifted to her nephew. "I'd like you to assist Rae with my duties regarding the ball."

Rubbing the back of his neck, Cole grimaced. "Tilly, you know I'm not really into the whole Christmas scene."

"I'm aware of that, but this is for charity. Children, no less. Foster kids like Rae's Maggie and Max."

Lowering his hand, he narrowed his curious gaze on Rae. "You have foster kids?"

Under his sudden scrutiny, she found herself squaring her shoulders. As if she were readying to go to battle. "I do."

"That's…commendable. It must be a challenge for a single woman such as yourself."

"At times. But I wouldn't trade it for the world."

Tilly eyed her nephew. "Please, Cole? You know I wouldn't ask if it wasn't important."

Returning his hands to his pockets, he rocked back on the heels of his dark brown oxfords and looked around the café, from the old wooden counter that had been there since the building was first used as a saloon in the 1800s to the exposed brick wall opposite. "You know it's impossible for me to tell you no."

The corners of Tilly's mouth tilted upward. "I was counting on that."

He nodded. "All right, what do you need me to do?"

"Oh, bless you, Cole." Tilly hugged and kissed him, a move that had his cheeks sporting a hint of pink. Stepping back, she said, "Okay, let's go over things."

While Tilly grabbed her green-cloth tote adorned with red and white snowflakes from a nearby chair, Rae struggled to wrap her brain around the whole situation. Before Tilly walked into the café, Rae had been ordering adorable red-and-black-plaid Christmas pajamas for her and the kids. She wanted this Christmas to be perfect for her little family. A family she'd longed for. But without Tilly here to help with the ball, that put more weight on Rae's shoulders, leaving less time for her holiday plans and threatening her perfect Christmas.

"I have every confidence the two of you can handle this." Tilly pulled a bulging three-inch red binder from the bag and plopped it on the wooden tabletop with a thud. "The bulk of the work is already done. You simply need to bring our plans to fruition." Setting one hand atop the binder, she smiled at Rae and Cole. "Everything you need to know to pull off a successful Mistletoe Ball is right in here."

Rae glanced at Cole, noting the color had drained from his clean-shaven face.

Waving them closer, Tilly continued. "Each colored tab denotes a different committee. The auctions, music, food, cleanup, et cetera. The chairs for each committee know their roles."

Rae eyed the woman. "What about the committees you chair?"

"The auctions, both live and silent, decorating and setup. But Adrian Hawkins co-chairs the live auction with me, so she'll be able to cover that."

"Does this mean we have to solicit donations for the silent auction?" Cole looked slightly horrified.

"No, dear. I've already done that. However, you will need to receive the items. Maybe pick up a few." Her gaze shifted to Rae. "You'll want to check in with the chairs every so often to make sure nothing slips through the cracks."

"Such as?" Rae squeaked out the words.

Again, Tilly placed a reverent hand on the binder. "It's all in here. Now, why don't the two of you go ahead and exchange phone numbers?"

"Why?" Rae and Cole asked at the same

time. Apparently, he wasn't any more enthused about this turn of events than Rae was.

"So you can contact each other, of course." Annoyance pinched the older woman's brow. "The first thing you need to do is sit down together and go through the binder. There are step-by-step instructions. Then, if you have any questions, make a list and call me."

Tilly acted as though heading up Bliss's biggest holiday event was as simple as throwing a child's birthday party. Step-by-step instructions were one thing, but if Rae knew anything about parties, it was to expect the unexpected. And that was what worried her most.

Suddenly queasy, she gripped the back of the nearest metal chair. Only minutes ago, she'd been planning the perfect Christmas. Now she was in charge of the town's biggest holiday celebration?

She'd made a commitment, though. Now she was stuck. Tilly's baby had been placed in Rae's less-than-capable hands. And she certainly didn't have high hopes when it came to Cole putting this year's Mistletoe Ball on the skids before it even began and leaving Rae's Christmas plans hanging in the balance. So there was only one thing she could do.

"We can meet tonight. My apartment upstairs." She eyed the handsome attorney. "Six thirty work for you?"

He studied her for a long moment. "I'll be there."

Eyeing the staircase at the back of the dining room, she added, "The café will be closed, so you'll have to use the outside stairs at the back of the building."

"So noted."

"Wonderful!" Tilly beamed. "I know you two will do a bang-up job."

Rae could only hope. Because from where she stood, the only things getting banged up were her Christmas plans. And if she disappointed Maggie and Max, she'd never forgive herself. Because, if her hopes of adoption fell through, she'd never get to make it up to them.

Cole Heinsohn turned off the lights in his office and stepped out into the darkened alley just before six thirty that evening, lamenting the whole spring forward, fall back concept. A week ago at this time, the last dregs of daylight would've still been visible.

He stowed his briefcase in his pickup before continuing up the alley to the back steps that led to Rae Girard's apartment.

Cole had never been able to say no to his aunt Tilly. She was one of the sweetest people he'd ever known, next to his mother, her late sister. Tilly was much more persistent, though. Still, agreeing to take her place as coordinator for the Mistletoe Ball had been a huge mistake.

Christmas wasn't his thing. Oh, he acknowledged the birth of Jesus our Lord and Savior, and thanked God for the greatest gift of all, but he tried to avoid most, if not all, of the celebrations. Sure, he'd gone through the motions for his mother and now Aunt Tilly whenever she insisted they get together, but otherwise, he preferred to use the day to catch up on paperwork at his office, knowing there would be no interruptions.

And yet Tilly had asked him to help with the biggest event of the Bliss holiday season. That was messed up.

No, you're the one who's messed up. Everyone else loves Christmas.

As he climbed the steps to Rae's apartment, he couldn't help thinking that living over her café didn't seem very practical now that she had children. With no yard, where did the kids go to run and play? He'd hated being cooped up in the house when he was little. Then again, the outside had been his escape. Thankfully, his father had been a rancher, so there had been plenty of space for Cole to escape to.

Taking a deep breath, he glanced up to see a

light shining from one of the windows on the second floor. That coupled with the fact that her SUV was parked next to the stairs told him Rae was indeed home.

May as well get this over with. The sooner he and Rae went over Tilly's notes, the sooner his aunt would stop pestering him.

He took the metal steps two at a time until he reached the six-by-eight landing adorned with potted plants and a welcome mat. Turning to his right, he rang the bell beside the solid-steel door.

A few seconds later, Rae pushed it open, looking a little frazzled. "Come on in." The words sounded more like a sigh.

He stepped inside the narrow space where hats, jackets and sweaters hung on wall hooks. "We did agree to meet at six thirty, didn't we?"

She considered him for a moment. "Yes, we did." After closing the door, she motioned for him to follow her, making a sharp left into a hallway where they passed a couple of bedrooms before spilling into a small eat-in kitchen with white cabinetry, wood floors and an exposed brick wall behind the pedestal dining table with four chairs. Opposite the table, ground beef sizzled in a skillet on the stainless-steel stove.

Picking up a wooden spoon, she gave the

meat a stir. "I don't know what I was thinking. The kids had dental appointments after school and, naturally, the dentist was running behind." With her free hand, she brushed a lock of brunette hair that had escaped her messy updo away from her face. "Now I'm just trying to get them fed and in bed at a decent hour."

Cole peered beyond the kitchen into the cozy living room with a wall of windows that overlooked the square. While a young girl with long, dark hair lay on the floor with her chin in her hands as she stared at a cartoon on the television, a little boy with olive skin and espresso eyes stood beside the leather sofa situated in front of the windows, glaring at Cole. His stare held a mixture of fear and warning, as though he didn't want Cole there.

"Look, Cole." He tore his gaze away from the boy as Rae set the spoon atop the light-colored granite and turned her bluer-than-blue eyes on him. "I know Tilly pretty much coerced you into helping with the ball, so I'm letting you off the hook. I can handle this on my own, no worries."

Between the boy and Rae, Cole found himself struggling to keep up. "I'm afraid I can't do that."

"Why not?" She perched a fist on her denim-covered hip. "It's obvious you don't *want* to help with the ball."

"No, but I promised Tilly, and I pride myself on being a man of my word."

"That's…commendable, but totally unnecessary. I promise to cover for you with Tilly."

Commendable? That was what he'd said about her being a foster parent. Had she thought he was minimizing her?

Straightening to his full six feet, an intimidation tactic that served him well in the courtroom, he narrowed his gaze on her. "Look, I don't know what sort of people you're used to dealing with, but I don't commit to things without intending to see them through."

Out of the corner of his eye, he saw the little boy scurry into the room. A split second later, he latched onto Rae, again glaring at Cole.

Obviously, the kid did not like him. And that was fine by Cole. He didn't do kids. Not that he disliked them; they just had a way of distracting one from their goal and, right now, his goal was to make Rae understand that he wasn't one to walk away from a commitment.

"All right, fine. We'll handle the ball together." Rae smoothed a hand over the boy's back. "But we're going to have to postpone this meeting."

"Just tell me when." Because Tilly would, no doubt, stay on him until they met.

"I've got my hands full prepping for the grand opening at Renwick Castle on Saturday, so I won't be available until Sunday afternoon or evening." She paused for a moment. "Are you planning to attend?"

"The grand opening? No." The entire town was invited, which equated to way too many people for his liking.

"You should, you know? It's where the Mistletoe Ball is going to take place. And since this will be the first year it's held there, it would give us the opportunity to get the lay of the land, so to speak."

Cole looked at the little boy watching him like a hawk. "I'll think about it."

Rae stooped to the boy's level. "Why don't you go watch TV with Maggie while I say goodbye to Mr. Cole?"

The boy seemed to tighten his grip and buried his face in her hip.

"It's okay, Max," she assured. "I'll be right back."

The kid looked up at her.

"It's okay, sweetie. I promise."

He glowered at Cole one last time before shuffling across the wood floor to drop beside the girl.

"I'll walk you out." Rae motioned toward the hall where they'd entered.

When they reached the door, she followed him outside. The evening air was comfortable without even a hint of a breeze.

Slipping her hands into the back pockets of her jeans, she looked up at him. "I'm sorry about Max. He and Maggie, his sister, came from an abusive environment, so he's rather skittish around men."

Abusive. The word slammed into Cole like a two-by-four being tossed around by a tornado. Now he understood why Max had kept staring at him. No telling what those dark eyes might have witnessed in the course of his short life.

"He's afraid I'm going to hurt you." A fact Cole should have picked up on sooner. Max was a foster child, after all. Now Cole found himself disgusted by the performance he'd put on inside. No wonder the boy had come running to Rae. He'd wanted to defend her.

"Something like that. Don't take it personally." Rae tried to wave it off, but it was far too personal to Cole to be dismissed. He recognized the pain in Max's eyes. Knew it all too well. And Cole couldn't stand to see a child living with the guilt and agony that had plagued him his entire life. A life spent mostly alone, steering clear of relationships for fear of turning out like his father.

No child should have to live like that. Now it was up to Cole to extend the olive branch.

"So, you're helping with the grand opening of Renwick Castle? Or should I say, the Bliss Texas History Museum and Event Center at Renwick Castle?"

She laughed then, and he couldn't help noticing how pretty her smile was. "I think I'll stick to Renwick Castle. The café is providing a chili supper for the event."

"I believe I've had your chili before. It was quite good."

"Thank you. I just hope I haven't bitten off more than I can chew. I mean, they've invited the entire town."

"I...could offer my assistance." Not that he relished the idea of mingling with townsfolk, but if it helped to prove himself a better person to Max, he'd be all in.

"But you're not going."

"That was before I heard you were serving chili."

"I see. I didn't realize you were such a fan."

"Well, it is fall." He shrugged. "Fall and chili go hand in hand."

"You're sure you're not just looking for a free meal?"

Shoving his hands in his pockets, he said, "Free, no. One I don't have to prepare? Perhaps."

Her grin set off a spark in her blue eyes. "At least you're honest."

"I should hope so." He nodded. "Until Saturday, then." He made his way down the stairs and into the night, determined to reach out to little Max. To find some way to be a positive influence in his life. But first he'd have to gain the boy's trust. And that was going to be a difficult row to hoe.

Chapter Two

Rae could hardly wait to crawl into bed.

But looking around the brand-new commercial kitchen of Renwick Castle on Saturday evening, she knew that wasn't happening anytime soon.

Scrubbing chili residue from the last stock pot just before eight o'clock, she still couldn't believe she'd pulled off such a large-scale event. While she'd been able to spread the food prep over the two weeks leading up to the castle's grand opening, serving upward of six hundred people nearly did her in. Evidently she wasn't as young as she used to be. Not that forty-four was old, but she didn't recall her feet aching this much before.

The door from what had once been the castle's dining room swung open.

"There you are." Her friend Paisley came

into the space, which was brimming with stainless-steel appliances and countertops. It was Paisley who'd had the dream of turning this once abandoned castle into an event center, unaware that Crockett Devereaux, the man who'd been a burr in her saddle for years, had also been vying for the forsaken structure to use as a museum. Yet in the end, the unlikely pair came together to achieve their dreams and, as of earlier today, they were engaged.

"Has this been a crazy day or what?" The statuesque redhead practically beamed as she retrieved a dish towel from the counter, despite having worked as hard, if not harder, than Rae.

"Crazy good, I'd say." Rae turned off the water and handed the pot to Paisley. "Not only has your dream of breathing new life into this castle finally come to fruition, you're getting married." Rae had been waiting all evening to celebrate with her friend. Now they squealed like a couple of teenagers.

"I still can't believe it." Paisley set the pot aside as Rae reached for her left hand to examine the engagement ring.

"It appears Crockett's taste in jewelry is as fine as his taste in women." Rae hugged her friend, who'd lost her husband and son in a tragic accident five years ago. Paisley deserved a second chance at love. Unlike Rae, who'd had her chance and blown it, Paisley's future had been stripped away from her.

She released Paisley, unable to stop smiling. "Any thoughts on when this union might take place?"

Her friend's sapphire eyes sparkled. "Well, obviously, we haven't had a chance to talk about it yet, but I'd be fine with a short engagement."

Rae lifted a brow. "How short?"

Paisley shrugged coyly. "A Christmas wedding might be lovely."

"Wow, that would be a short engagement."

"Not as short as Christa and Mick's," Paisley reminded her. Their friend, who owned the local hardware store, had been engaged less than a week before saying "I do" earlier this year.

"Just be sure to let me know ASAP. Between the kids' stuff and the Mistletoe Ball, I might be in over my head."

Paisley leaned against the counter. "Speaking of the Mistletoe Ball, I couldn't help noticing that Tilly's nephew, Cole, was helping you today."

"Yeah." Rae was still surprised, not to mention curious, as to why he'd had such a sudden change of heart about attending the event. Despite his claim the other night, she was pretty sure it had nothing to do with her chili. Yet he'd been one of the first to arrive. He'd even managed to talk Maggie and Max into helping him pass out bags of corn chips—something Max seemed happy to do, though he stuck close to her the entire time, still wary of Cole.

"Tilly had to leave town indefinitely, so I'm now in charge of the ball and she tasked Cole with helping me."

"That's an interesting turn of events, though it doesn't explain why he was helping you." Her friend had a glimmer in her eye that Rae recognized all too well.

After watching her friends Laurel, Christa and Paisley fall in love over the past year and a half, Rae knew they'd all be more than happy to see her follow in their footsteps. But Rae wasn't about to travel that road. When her husband walked out of her life and into the arms of another woman, Rae vowed she'd never fall in love again. And that was a promise she intended to keep.

"Frankly, I have no idea why he offered to help." She pulled the plug from the sink. "But I wasn't about to turn him down. And knowing there was an extra set of eyes watching Maggie and Max was beneficial, too."

"Speaking of which, where are those two?"

"Mackenzie asked if she could show them the ballroom." Crockett's twelve-year-old daughter had been keeping the two entertained while

Rae cleaned up. And Max loved playing with her eight-year-old brother, David. "Something about sock skating."

"Ah, yes. That's the kids' favorite pastime when they're here."

The door swung open again and Cole paused when he spotted Paisley. "Am I interrupting?" He was wearing his trademark suit and button-down, though he'd loosened his tie.

"Not at all." A grinning Paisley motioned him into the kitchen.

His silver-gray eyes sought out Rae. "Is there anything I can help you with?"

She looked around the space. "No, I think I'm finally done."

"In that case, would you care to join me in the ballroom so we can discuss the Mistletoe Ball?"

She'd rather go home and crawl into bed, but since she was the one who'd suggested they check things out… "May as well. The kids are up there anyway."

After ascending the grand staircase to the second floor with Paisley in tow, they found all four kids sliding across the ballroom in their sock feet.

"Mama Rae, look at me." Max glided across the polished wood floor while crystal chandeliers gleamed overhead.

"Very good, Max." Her heart sank a little

when Maggie didn't acknowledge her. Rae still didn't have a good read on the girl. There were times when she was bubbly and friendly with Rae and other times she seemed to withdraw inside herself and ignore Rae altogether.

"I thought I might find you here."

The adults all turned at the sound of Crockett's voice.

A smile split Paisley's pretty face as her intended approached. "I was wondering when I'd see you again. Did you get all the tables and chairs squared away?" Though guests were able to tour the castle today, the grounds had been the main gathering place, with beautifully decorated tables spread across the property.

"With Cole and your father helping, the job was completed in a third of the time." He slid an arm around Paisley's waist and pulled her close. "By the way, your folks went on back to your place."

"I'm surprised they made it this long."

Suddenly uncomfortable, Rae said, "Cole and I were about to explore the ballroom. The Mistletoe Ball is being held here, so we thought we'd scope things out."

Crockett smirked in Cole's direction. "How did you get roped into that?"

"An unexpected turn of events had Tilly relinquishing her duties to me."

"Actually, I have some ideas, if you'd like to hear them." Paisley looked from Rae to Cole.

Given that Paisley had been in the wedding planning business for years, Rae said, "We're all ears."

While Paisley wandered around, going into detail about table and dance floor layout, the children's laughter grew quiet, and Max sought out Rae. She happily lifted him into her arms, stroking his back while he laid his head on her shoulder, all the while continuing to follow her friend. He was such a sweet boy.

"We'll already have a Christmas tree in place—" Paisley motioned in the general area of the windows "—so that will cut down on the need for decorations."

"For sure," said Rae. "I think centerpieces will suffice."

"What do you have in mind?"

Rae relayed Tilly's idea of wood disks adorned with hurricane candleholders, cedar boughs and pinecones.

Beside her, Cole cleared his throat. "I think we might need to wrap up this discussion."

Rae looked up at him. "Problem?"

"Maggie and Max are both crashed." He pointed across the room where Maggie lay curled up on the floor, using her jacket for a pillow.

"Oh, sweet girl." Only then did she realize Max had gone limp in her arms. "Let me put him in the car and I'll come back for Maggie."

"I can carry her." Cole seemed to catch himself then. "I mean, if you don't mind."

"No, not at all." Though she was definitely surprised. "Thank you."

The night air was cool but not cold as they strapped the kids into the back seat of her SUV.

Rae opened the driver's door. "I appreciate your help. Now I just have to figure out how to get them both upstairs to my apartment."

"I'd be happy to follow you and carry one of them."

Ugh. Her comment had made it sound as though she wanted his assistance. "That's not necessary. I was just thinking out loud. Not gunning for help."

"I understand. But you can't carry both of them at once. And even though Bliss is a small town, leaving a sleeping child in the car alone isn't the best idea."

"No, I don't suppose it is." Still, she didn't like the idea of being indebted to him. And after the way he'd pitched in to help today, she didn't want him to think she was taking advantage of him, either. "Okay, but your next two meals at the café are on the house."

He lifted a brow. "Only two?"

"Oh, so now you're looking for some free meals. Wait—" she gripped the door tighter "—you were joking, weren't you?"

The corners of his mouth tilted upward. "Yes."

"And I'm more tired than I thought." She threw herself into the driver's seat. "See you in a few."

He followed her to her place, then scooped Max from the passenger side while Rae grabbed Maggie. Once inside her apartment, she led him to the kids' room. After tucking Maggie in, she watched as Cole settled Max into his bed. He removed the boy's shoes and covered him with his dinosaur comforter. Then he brushed his fingers across Max's forehead.

"Good night, Max." His whispered words sent goose bumps up Rae's arms.

She'd have never imagined Cole Heinsohn would have such a tender heart for kids.

She closed the door halfway as they stepped into the hall. "Thank you again. You made what could have been a difficult transition very easy for me."

"Now you can get some rest." He strolled toward the door. "By the way, my aunt has been texting me all day, wanting to know when we're going to tackle that binder of hers."

Pausing at the door, Rae said, "She can be a little pushy sometimes."

"A little?"

Despite being exhausted, she chuckled. "That's why she puts on such a successful event. She knows what she wants and knows how to get it done."

"And now she's put us in charge."

"No pressure, right?"

"Well, she's going to keep hounding us until we sit down and go over things. So, if you could give me a day and time, I might be able to hold her off temporarily."

Rae yawned. "The café is closed on Sundays. Are you available tomorrow afternoon, say around three?"

"I am."

"I'll meet you here, then."

"Sounds good." He opened the door and stepped outside. "Sleep well, Rae." With that, he descended the steps and waved as he climbed into his truck.

Rae watched the handsome attorney drive away, feeling more than a little perplexed. She understood his commitment to his aunt, admired it even. But why had he been so insistent on helping Rae today, particularly where Maggie and Max were concerned? It didn't fit the image of the man who was usually quite distant.

Glancing up at the stars, she couldn't help wondering what had changed. And she was going to do her best to find out exactly what that was.

Cole had hoped to make some inroads with little Max yesterday, but judging by the way the boy seemed to go on high alert whenever Cole was near, it was going to be a long haul. All he could do was work toward earning the boy's trust. And Cole knew from experience how difficult trust was going to be for Max. If Cole hadn't had Uncle Gary, Tilly's husband, in his life, he might have grown up expecting all men to be as mean and angry as his father.

Had Max ever had anyone he could trust? Or had he lived his whole life fearing men?

Turning his truck into the alley behind Rae's place, Cole realized he'd actually enjoyed himself yesterday. Working alongside Maggie and Max as they passed out chips had been rather entertaining. The banter between brother and sister was comical at times. All in all, it wasn't a bad way to spend a beautiful fall afternoon. Though interacting with so many people had been a tad overwhelming for someone who preferred a more reclusive lifestyle.

He'd grown accustomed to his solitary life. He had his work to keep him busy. Life in a small town meant he handled everything from family law to criminal defense to civil litigation, estate practice and property transactions. In other words, he'd seen it all. The good, the bad, and the unsavory sides of life.

Then there was his father. Or at least the man who resided in his father's body. Dementia had turned Leland Heinsohn into someone unfamiliar to Cole. The man who'd been perpetually enraged for most of Cole's life was now kind and jovial, laughing off things that once would've had him taking out his frustration on Cole's mother.

Though his father no longer recognized him, Cole still visited the man a few times a week. In part for appearances, but mostly because he knew his mother would be disappointed if he didn't. Strangely enough, for as much as he dreaded the visits, he actually enjoyed the old man's company. But reconciling the man he was now with the man he'd once been was something Cole still struggled with.

Shaking off the morose thoughts, he pulled his truck alongside Rae's SUV. If they didn't dive into Tilly's binder today, he'd never get his aunt off his back. For the past three days, she'd been texting him reminders morning, noon and night. It was enough to make him crazy.

He stepped out of his truck and into a perfect autumn day. Temps in the low seventies had him rolling up the sleeves of his plaid shirt as he made his way up the steps.

Rae pushed the door open a few seconds after he knocked but seemed to stop in her tracks as her blue eyes moved from his head to his well-worn boots. "You're not wearing a suit."

He glanced at his faded Wranglers. "No, not today."

"Oh." As she clung to the door, he couldn't help noticing a hint of glitter on her face. "I just… I've never seen you in anything but a suit."

"I don't usually wear a suit when I'm hanging around the house."

"No." She continued to stare, looking almost dumbfounded. "I don't suppose you would."

For whatever reason, he found her reaction rather cute. "May I come in?"

"Yes." She pushed the door wide and waited for him to pass.

Inside, the sound of children's laughter echoed down the hall, along with the pitter-patter of small feet on the wooden floor.

"Sounds like they're having fun," he said as Rae whisked past him.

She groaned. "They've been like this all day. I had them decorating some pinecones for Christmas, but they lost interest in that pretty quick."

That explained the glitter. "Isn't it a little early to be thinking about Christmas?" Not that he ever put any effort into the holiday. The only tree he put up was at the office and only because his assistant, Brenda, insisted on it. Still, Christmas was more than a month away.

"Are you kidding?" They reached the kitchen and Rae glared at him as if he'd sprouted horns. "I started preparing weeks ago."

Great. She was one of *those* people. The kind who watched Christmas movies in July and put the tree up the moment the Thanksgiving turkey was eaten, if not before. No wonder she and Tilly got along.

Eager to change the subject, he eyed Maggie and Max racing back and forth in the living room. The windows were open wide, allowing the fresh air to spill inside.

"They look a little restless. Can't say I blame them. This is one of those days when you don't want to be stuck inside."

"Typically, I'd take them to the park, but I don't think that would be very conducive to our meeting."

"And two restless kids running around is?" Realizing how his comment might have come across, as though he was complaining about the kids, he added, "I'm up for the park if you are."

"Are you sure?" Skepticism had her wrinkling her nose.

"It's a beautiful day. Why not?"

"Okay. Don't say I didn't warn you, though."

He watched as she filled a backpack with water bottles, snacks and sunglasses.

"Don't forget your jackets!" Rae hollered. "Just in case."

The whole scene only confirmed his thoughts on how inconvenient it must be to live over the café.

But Rae didn't seem to be complaining. So he'd keep his thoughts to himself.

"You're welcome to ride with us," said Rae when they finally made it downstairs to their vehicles.

He didn't mind. But one look at Max, and Cole knew it was a bad idea. "I'll just take my truck." That way he could leave whenever he was ready.

When the two cars reached the park on the other side of town, the kids practically bolted from Rae's vehicle and ran straight for the playground and the swings.

"I think bringing them here was a good decision." Cole took the binder from Rae and fell into step alongside her as she followed the kids, albeit at a more leisurely pace.

"They like coming here." She dropped the backpack atop a picnic table. "Thank you for agreeing."

Why was she thanking him? "From what you've told me, they've had a rough life. It's time they're allowed to be kids."

She smiled up at him. "My thoughts exactly." Eyeing the binder in his hand, she said, "Shall we get started?"

He joined her on the bench that afforded them full view of the kids. They'd made it through the duties of two committees when Maggie called out to Rae from the bottom of one of the slides—the larger one.

"Max is afraid to climb up the slide."

Rae sucked in a breath. "Max wants to keep up with his sister, but he has a little fear of heights."

"In his defense, that slide probably looks like a skyscraper to him." Cole stretched his legs out in front of him as a lone cloud momentarily dimmed the sun.

"I know. But I made the mistake of going down it with him once and now he won't go without me."

"You know that's not safe, right?"

"Yes, but I didn't know what else to do."

"I used to be afraid of heights. Do you think he'd listen if I tried to coach him through it?"

She lifted a shoulder. "Go for it. I'll stay here so he's less tempted to defer to me."

"Smart thinking." Cole stood and made his way across the wood mulch–covered playground to where Max stared up the steps of the slide.

"Kind of scary looking, isn't it?"

The boy's gaze jerked to Cole and he took a step back.

When he was a few feet from the boy, Cole crouched, putting him at the same height as Max and, hopefully, appearing less intimidating.

"I remember the first big slide I went on. I was afraid, too."

"I'm not afraid," said Max.

"You're a lot braver than I was. I couldn't climb those steps until someone walked up behind me."

The boy looked from Cole to the top of the slide as Maggie approached.

"You can do it, Maxy," she said. "Just watch me." She wrapped a hand around each of the side rails then hurried to the top before looking down at her brother. "See, it's easy."

"Good job, Maggie." Cole turned his attention to Max. "Would you like me to walk up the steps behind you?"

The boy's gaze fell to the ground. He toed at the mulch with his sneaker. At least he was considering Cole's offer. *Lord, please let him trust me.*

"That was fun!" Maggie hollered when she reached the bottom of the curly slide.

"What do you say, Max?" Cole kept his focus on the boy. "Shall we give it a try?"

A moment later, Max nodded and turned for the ladder.

Cole fell in behind him, gripping the side rails so he practically enveloped Max with his body. "Okay, you start climbing and I'll be right behind you the whole way."

After a slight hesitation, Max lifted one foot and moved it to the next step, then did it again and again.

Hope swelled within Cole. "You're doing great, Max. I'm right behind you."

"I did it!" the kid cheered when he reached the top. He settled his little bottom onto the slide.

"You sure did." Cole patted him on the shoulder. "Now you get yourself down that slide and I'll meet you at the bottom."

"You're not coming with me?"

"Sorry, champ, I'm too big. But you've got

this. Sliding is the easy part. And I'll be right there at the bottom when you get there, all right?"

Again Max hesitated. Finally he said, "Okay." He pushed off and Cole made a hasty escape from the ladder, leaping once he was halfway down so he could be there to celebrate when Max reached the bottom. And though his foot twisted on landing, Cole still made it in time.

"Yay, Max!" Maggie cheered.

Rae was there, too. "Max, I'm so proud of you." She hugged him as he stood.

"That was fun!" The boy beamed as he looked up at Cole. "Can we do it again?"

Ignoring the ache in his foot, he said, "Sure, we can." This time was as successful as the first, only faster. And Cole didn't jump this go-round.

By his third attempt, Max was ready to fly solo, though Cole stood at the bottom of the ladder, just in case.

"I did it all by myself!" The grin on Max's face warmed Cole's heart.

"Way to go, champ." Noting that the sun was rapidly slipping toward the western horizon, Cole added, "I think this is cause for celebration. What would you all say to some pizza?"

"Yay!" Brother and sister cheered in unison. Then he caught Rae's stare and realized that in his excitement he'd failed to clear things with her. "That is, if your mom says it's all right."

Her gaze drifted to his foot. "Did we twist our ankle?"

"Ah, it's nothing." At least, nothing an ice pack and some Tylenol wouldn't take care of.

Arms crossed, she met his gaze again. "You know, we really didn't accomplish anything."

"Maybe not where the ball is concerned, but do you see those smiling faces?" He pointed to the kids. "If they're happy, I'm happy."

Rae continued to watch him. "But that won't get Tilly off of our backs. So, if we hope to make any headway, we should take said pizza back to my apartment so we can discuss the ball while we eat."

He nodded. "Pizza at your apartment it is then."

"*With* a side of ice for your foot."

"If you say so."

"I do. The ice is nonnegotiable. I've got enough on my plate without a heaping helping of guilt added to it."

"We can't have that."

"If we're in agreement, then, counselor, you've got yourself a deal."

Chapter Three

This was getting ridiculous. Seemed no matter how hard they tried—okay, so they hadn't tried *that* hard—Rae and Cole couldn't seem to squeeze in enough time to make it through Tilly's big binder.

Emptying the contents of her backpack, Rae placed the unopened water bottles in the refrigerator and tucked the fruit snacks in the cupboard while the kids played in their room. Apparently, the promise of pizza was a good motivator. It certainly motived her. Her stomach grumbled as she removed the tray holding paint, glue, glitter and pinecones from the table. Then tightened when she recalled the sight of Cole limping to his truck. And yet she'd let him pick up the pizzas.

How unsympathetic could she be? And after the way he'd helped Max overcome his fear.

Despite having said she'd stay on the bench, once the two had approached the slide, she'd sneaked closer, her camera at the ready. She'd heard how Cole used his own experience to embolden Max. Seen the tender look in his eyes as he'd done so.

She never would have imagined the matter-of-fact attorney would have a soft spot for a little boy struggling to break free from his past. A past littered with scenes of violence that still woke Max up in the middle of the night.

Rae shook her head. Why Maggie and Max's mother hadn't left her abusive husband was a mystery to her. Perhaps if she had, she wouldn't have died at the hands of the man who purported to love her. And little Max wouldn't have been there to witness it.

A notification on her phone had her shaking off the miserable thoughts.

Your order of Santa's Workshop Christmas Pajamas has shipped.

"Yes!" If she'd waited until after Thanksgiving to place her order, they likely would have been sold out. Only one of many reasons she'd begun her shopping early. The perfect Christmas wasn't something that just happened, it took planning and preparation. Just like the

Mistletoe Ball. And if she and Cole didn't get a handle on things soon, both the ball and her perfect Christmas would be in jeopardy.

As the sun set on a gorgeous day, a chill sifted through her front windows. She hurried into the living room to close them, tiptoeing around monster trucks and troll dolls. Only then did she remember the doll Maggie had mentioned the other day. She'd better jump on that soon, lest she miss out. Because the last thing she wanted to see on Christmas morning was a disappointed child.

The doorbell rang as she closed the last window, so she hurried back across the living room, through the kitchen, nearly running into Maggie in the hall.

"Pizza's here!" The girl jumped up and down.

Evidently, they'd all worked up an appetite.

Rae opened the door to see Cole holding two pizza boxes. She still couldn't get over seeing him without a suit. She never would have taken him for a boots and jeans kind of guy. He pulled it off very well, though. Made him look more approachable.

"As you requested," he said as he limped inside. "One supreme and one cheese pizza."

"I can hardly wait." Rae pulled the door closed. "Now I just need to get that ice pack."

"I'm starbing." Maggie followed Cole.

"Max?" Rae poked her head into the kids' room as she passed and found him on the floor, playing with some action figures. "Pizza's here. Time to come eat." When he didn't acknowledge her, she added, "Now, please."

After a quick detour into the bathroom to grab an ice pack, she returned to the kitchen and pulled a couple of ice trays from the freezer.

"Gracious, that pizza smells good," she said as she put the cubes into the bag.

"Where are your plates?" Cole was beside her now.

"I'll get them. You sit down. And grab that extra chair in the corner there to prop your foot on. I'll have this pack ready in a jiff, so you may as well settle in."

"Anyone ever tell you you're kind of bossy?"

Her heart squeezed. Sean, her ex-husband, had accused her of that same thing. Strange how the take-charge attitude that had attracted him to her had ended up being her downfall. He'd said he wanted a wife, not a mother. She knew better, though. Sean was never satisfied. Whether it was cars, houses or wives, he always seemed to be on the lookout for something better.

"If a situation calls for it, yes. And like I said, I don't need the guilt."

Noting that Max still hadn't made it to the table, she called for him once again.

He shuffled into the room about the time she handed the ice pack to Cole. Instead of taking his seat, though, he latched onto Rae and hid behind her.

"What's up, Max?" She looked down at him. "Aren't you hungry?"

He didn't respond. Instead, he simply glared at Cole.

Don't tell me we're back to this. They seemed to be doing so well at the park.

She scooted his chair beside hers and sat. "Come on. You can sit beside me." She patted his seat and waited for him to comply. When he didn't, she added, "Would you rather go back to your room?"

Still scowling at Cole, he shook his head and said, "I don't want him here."

Embarrassment tangled with frustration, deflating her. "But you had so much fun with Mr. Cole at the park. He helped you learn to do the slide all by yours—"

"Stop, Rae." She turned to see Cole stand. Now who was being bossy? "It's all right. If Max doesn't want me here, I'll go. I don't want him to be uneasy in his own home."

She was in a no-win situation. And she hated it. Hated that Max and Maggie's father had robbed Max of the ability to trust. *God, I really need some help down here.*

When Cole pushed in his chair, she stood. "You can at least take some of this pizza." He'd paid for it, after all. She pulled out three slices before closing the lid. Then she grabbed the box and accompanied him to the door.

"I'm really sorry about this."

"Don't be." He took hold of the box as he stepped outside. "It's not your fault. It's not Max's, either. He's obviously working through a lot of things. There's no need to push him."

Holding on to the door handle, she said, "But we're supposed to be working on the Mistletoe Ball. That means we're going to have to be together whether he likes it or not."

"Maybe so. But not tonight. We had fun at the park. Let's just leave it at that."

She knew he was right, but that didn't mean she had to like it.

"Now, if you'll excuse me, I have a date with an ice pack and a football game."

"Smart man."

He gestured with the pizza box. "Good night, Rae."

"Good night." Sadness washed over her as she watched him make his way down the steps in a gingerly manner.

God, give me strength. Please help Max and

Maggie heal. And please, please, don't let me mess up the Mistletoe Ball.

Cole limped out of the courthouse Monday afternoon, annoyed that he hadn't had enough sense to wear his boots today. At least they'd have given his ankle some support. Now he was eager to get back to his office and that bottle of ibuprofen waiting inside his desk drawer. If only it would help the ache in his heart.

How was he going to earn Max's trust?

Pausing at a nearby bench, Cole blew out a long breath. Since leaving Rae's yesterday, he'd been haunted by the sad eyes of a little boy who longed to be normal. But the memories of a tormented past held Max captive, sentencing him to a life plagued with fear and uncertainty.

The sun peered through the live oak leaves that danced overhead. By all counts, this was a perfect fall day. Would Rae be taking Maggie and Max to the park again? Not that Cole would be joining them.

He eased onto the bench to give his foot a rest. Yesterday, he'd foolishly found himself believing that Max had opened the door just a crack, giving Cole hope that he'd be able to forge a friendship with the boy. A morsel of something that might help set Max on a road to normalcy. So the kid's deep desire to see Cole gone last night had felt like a gut punch.

He knew he shouldn't take Max's rejection so personally. That it wasn't Max's fault—but the heartbreak was there, nonetheless. Still, Cole refused to force the situation, so he'd left. Not because he'd wanted to, but out of respect for Max's feelings. And even though Max was too young to understand that, perhaps it would play a role in helping him realize that maybe Cole wasn't a bad guy after all.

If only Max had had an Uncle Gary. Someone even-tempered, thoughtful and always quick with a smile. Cole wanted that for Max so badly, he could almost taste it. The realization that not all men lashed out in anger would go a long way toward helping Max heal.

For as much as Cole would like to be that man, he knew he probably wasn't the right person for the job. The fear of hurting someone, even if it was verbally and emotionally the way his father had repeatedly hurt Cole and his mother, was why Cole kept most everyone at arm's length. He hadn't dated since college when a young lady had falsely accused him of assault. Thankfully, witnesses had corroborated Cole's story and there'd been no charges, but it had left him with a strong determination not to put himself in that position again. And yet he now found himself working with the beautiful café owner to appease his aunt Tilly.

His gaze inadvertently drifted beyond the row of cars and trucks parked at an angle along the square and across the street to the café. Perhaps what happened with Max last night was God's way of telling Cole he shouldn't be spending so much time with Rae. Because, to Cole's chagrin, he actually enjoyed being with her. She was down to earth and unassuming. The simple fact that she was a foster mom spoke volumes about her character. Add to that how she obviously adored Max and Maggie, and had a heart to help them overcome their past, and…well, that made her incredibly attractive. And that didn't bode well for Cole.

No, the quicker they could get through the Mistletoe Ball, the quicker he could move on down the road and away from Rae. How was that ever going to happen, though, when something always seemed to disrupt their plans?

Perhaps God was trying to send him a message. Maybe he should just back off. Relegate his involvement to the power of prayer over Max's life.

"Cole?" The sound of Rae's voice only added to his turmoil.

He turned to see her approach. She wore jeans with a black Rae's Fresh Start Café T-shirt and her shoulder-length waves were pinned up, though a few brunette locks framed her pretty face. He couldn't help noticing how tremulous her smile was as she continued across the walk.

"Is everything okay?" She paused beside the bench, her blue eyes drifting to his outstretched leg. "Is your foot still hurting?"

"Just a little residual pain. Nothing to be concerned about."

"Did you put ice on it?"

"I did. And you'll be happy to know there's no swelling." Well, not much, anyway. Not enough to cause her worry. She had enough to deal with.

"That's good." Crossing her arms, she looked from his foot to a pot of yellow mums and then across the street, without ever making eye contact. "I, um, I was planning to stop by your office."

"Oh?" He straightened, curiosity niggling. Rae had never visited his office before. Could it be that she wanted to re-extend her offer to handle the Mistletoe Ball on her own, without his help? At this point, it would probably make things easier for her. He'd find some way to tell Tilly.

Finally, she looked down at him. "Mind if I join you?" Yep, she was going to give him the old heave-ho, all right.

He gestured to the space beside him, an unfamiliar surge of anxiety settling in his chest. Why was he nervous? He didn't get nervous.

Once seated, she rubbed her hands over her thighs, as if her palms were sweaty. Was she trying to come up with a way to let him down gently? "I want to apologize for Max's behavior last night."

"That's not necessary." He leaned forward, resting his elbows on his knees as he watched an elderly couple shuffle arm in arm toward the courthouse. "Max is struggling. I get that."

"He was also very tired last night. He barely finished his first slice of pizza before nodding off at the table." She was trying to make Cole feel better. As if, somehow, Max's behavior was a reflection on her. "And then, this morning, he couldn't seem to stop talking about you."

Cole faced her now, unable to hide his surprise. "Really?"

"He went on and on about how big and brave you were and how you helped him be brave so he could go down the slide."

Something inside Cole shifted. "He said that?"

She nodded. "Not only that, he asked if you could go to the park with us again so he could slide. When I reminded him of how he'd behaved at dinner, how he treated you, he hung his little head, that bottom lip pooching out, and said he was sorry."

An unexpected lump formed in Cole's throat, but he cleared it away. "I'm sorry he's so conflicted about me." Yet Cole understood it. He remembered going to a friend's seventh birthday party and watching the boy's jovial father like a hawk, wondering when he'd start yelling the way Cole's father always had.

"Please know that it's not you, Cole. Max is very cautious of all men."

"So you've said." He leaned back against the metal slats of the bench. "Abuse impacts kids more than people realize. I'm just glad to see that Maggie is doing so well."

Rae's countenance fell briefly. "Oh, she has her moments. But things are different for her because she was—" Rae's eyes drifted to the canopy of trees as she blinked rapidly "—at school when their father killed their mother."

Cole's heart stopped. If Maggie was at school, where was—

"Max wasn't so fortunate, though." Rae again looked his way. "He was at home. A neighbor called the police about a gunshot. They found Max hiding in a closet."

An odd and unwelcome wave of sorrow, pain and anger washed over Cole. As an attorney, he'd heard all about the uglier side of humanity in many a courtroom and remained unmoved. But at the moment, he was barely holding himself together. Whether it was because he used to hide in his closet, too, trying to escape the sound of his father's yelling, or the simple fact that Max's father had robbed his son of his innocence, Cole couldn't be certain, yet there was one thing he knew for sure. Max deserved to be happy and carefree. To live without fear that something bad was going to happen to him or someone he loved. To be a kid with dreams of a bright future.

And Cole would do anything he could to ensure that happened. He didn't know what it might look like, but he would not give up on Max.

With hope coursing through his veins, he looked at Rae. "What time should I be at the park?"

Chapter Four

Rae pulled her SUV alongside the curb at the park later that afternoon, noting the gray cloud bank to the northwest that promised rain. She could only pray it would hold off until the kids were done playing. Cole had seemed beyond willing to give Max another chance, something Rae was more than grateful for, so she'd hate to see their time cut short. She just hoped Max wouldn't have another change of heart.

Turning off the engine, she unbuckled her seat belt, eyeing the two adorable children in her back seat. They had truly amplified her life and she thanked God for them each and every day. How she prayed they'd one day be hers forever.

She reached for the door handle. "Who's ready to play?"

"I am!" Maggie hurried to unbuckle herself from the rear passenger seat.

"Me, too." Max wiggled as Rae hastily exited the vehicle to assist him with his harness.

Pausing at the curb, Maggie glanced over her shoulder. "Race you to the slide."

"No fair!" Max squirmed even more, kicking his legs and sending a pout in Rae's direction as his sister closed her door. "Mama Rae, make her stop."

"Now, don't get so upset, Max." She didn't want that, especially with Cole promising to meet them—something she'd kept to herself just in case he changed his mind. "I'm sure she was just teasing. She always waits for you." Rae unhooked him before checking on his sister. To her surprise, Maggie was halfway across the playground. That wasn't like her. She was usually very considerate of Max's feelings.

Rae cupped her hands around her mouth. "Margaret Sophia, you need to come back here right now!"

The girl stopped and looked back at her for a long moment before obeying. The hesitation was out of character for the normally compliant child.

Holding Max's hand, Rae continued on to the sidewalk and waited for Maggie as she shuffled toward them.

Rae crouched as she approached. "Would you care to tell me what that was all about?" She took extra care to remain calm and not raise her voice. "Not only was I in no position to watch you, you shouldn't call a race and then take off before your brother is even out of the car."

Maggie's ebony eyes bore into Rae. "I was just kidding."

"Max didn't know that, and he was very upset."

The girl's gaze drifted to her brother.

Still taken aback by Maggie's unusual behavior, Rae added, "I think you owe us an apology."

Maggie focused on the ground. "Sorry."

"Why's everyone standing around?" Cole's voice had all three of them whipping their heads to see him strolling across the grass, the sun highlighting his hint of a smile. Only then did Rae spot his truck parked on the street opposite her vehicle.

Standing, she couldn't help noticing the delight on both kids' faces. Especially Max's, which eased Rae's fears.

When she turned her attention to Cole, she noticed he'd not only ditched his suit coat but he'd traded his oxfords for cowboy boots. That seemed totally fitting for an attorney in a small rural community like Bliss.

"Who wants to slide?" He looked from Max to Maggie.

"I do!" they cheered in unison, bouncing up and down.

He cut a glance in Rae's direction. "Care to join us?"

Grateful for a moment to collect her thoughts, she said, "I'll be there in a minute." She watched them walk away, pleased to see Max actually engaging with Cole, even if he was rather subdued.

Opening the passenger door of her SUV, she retrieved Tilly's massive binder. Tilly had texted earlier, wanting to know how things were coming along. Rae had simply informed her that they were progressing. Even if it was at a snail's pace. And while she doubted they'd accomplish anything today, at least she'd be prepared in case they got a few moments to discuss the ball.

A couple minutes later, she approached a picnic table not far from where the kids were playing, watching a beaming Max zip down the slide for a second time. When he reached the bottom, he hopped off and hurried around to the steps where Cole waited. Yet as Cole stepped up to assist him, Max shook his head and pushed the man away.

The move had Rae dropping the binder on the table and heading their way at a brisk pace, fearful Max was shunning Cole again.

Out of the corner of her eye, she noticed a couple of boys riding bicycles nearby as Cole neared her. "What happened?"

He dragged a hand through his thick hair. "Apparently, my services are no longer needed."

Her gaze searched his, her muscles tightening. "Why not?"

The handsome attorney shrugged. "He says he wants to do it himself."

"You're kidding?"

"Nope. He's gained the confidence he needed to overcome his fears."

Watching a squirrel shimmy up a nearby oak tree, she breathed a sigh of relief. "All because of you."

Cole shrugged. "Perhaps." He acted so modest, but his grin told her just how much it meant to him.

"In that case—" she faced him "—I guess we have time to dig into Tilly's binder."

"Do we have to?"

"Yes. She texted me today."

"Okay, but it won't be nearly as fun as helping Max."

His comment made her feel all warm and fuzzy inside. "I know, adulting is overrated."

"So when is the setup for the ball?" he asked a short time later as they were discussing setup and decorations.

"The night before. We'll do the decorating then, too."

His brow pinched. "Trust me, I'm better at setup than decorating."

"Fine by me. I'll be more than happy to let you do the heavy lifting." She paused. "I'm sure we'll have help, though. Paisley and Crockett are bound to be there. And if I know my friend, she'll make things feel more like a party."

A shout cut through the warm afternoon air.

Rae jerked her head up as Cole rose.

Maggie stood beside her brother, who was on the ground near the swings while two older boys towered over him.

Cole sprinted toward the group as Rae hurried to catch up.

"What's going on here?" Cole looked from the older boys to Maggie while Rae scooped Max into her arms.

"They were being mean to us." Maggie was more than a little emphatic.

"He tried to kick us." One of the older boys pointed at Max.

"They said I was just a stupid girl." While Maggie's voice cracked, she held her own.

Placing a hand on Maggie's shoulder, Cole looked at the two boys. "How old are you? Nine? Ten?"

The older boy puffed out his chest. "I'm ten. He's only eight." He poked a thumb toward the younger one.

Cole's stare narrowed on the bigger boy. "I see. So, do you two enjoy making fun of kids who are younger than you?"

The duo looked at each other, their faces suddenly pale.

Cole crossed his arms, a move that made him more intimidating. "Let me ask you this. Did anyone ever make fun of you when you were their age?"

The older boy scuffed his sneaker over the wood chips. "My big brother makes fun of me all the time."

"I'm sorry to hear that." Cole was the epitome of calm, cool and collected. "It probably hurts your feelings, doesn't it?"

The boy shrugged, refusing to make eye contact.

"He really doesn't like it when his brother punches him," said the younger boy.

Still holding Max tight, Rae found her heart

going out to the boy as she contemplated what his home life might be like.

After studying the boys a moment longer, Cole said, "It's important to treat others the way you'd like to be treated." His gaze moved to the gray clouds that had drifted closer, adding a chill to the late-afternoon air. "You two go on home now."

As the boys hopped on their bikes and rode away, Rae heaved a sigh of relief and looked at Cole. "I'm so glad you were here. There's no way I would have been as calm as you were." On the contrary, she probably would have gone all Mama Bear, and Max and Maggie didn't need to see that.

"I'm an attorney. I get paid to be cool under pressure."

"Well, I think you handled the situation with a lot of grace. Hopefully, your words hit home with them."

He lifted a shivering Maggie into his arms as the wind kicked up. "Shall we play a while longer or are you guys ready to head home?"

"I want to go home." Maggie snuggled closer.

Rae looked at the sky. "That's probably a good idea since the weather's about to turn. That chicken and dumplings I planned for dinner sounds even better now that the temps are dropping."

Max lifted his head from her shoulder to look at her. "Can Mr. Cole eat chicken dumplings with us?"

Rae saw the way Cole's eyes widened ever so slightly. "That's fine by me. Why don't you ask him, Max?"

The boy's dark gaze met Cole's. "Will you? Please?"

"You and Mama Rae could do some more work." Arms around Cole's neck, Maggie watched him.

The unflappable attorney's mouth twitched as the corners lifted ever so slightly. Giving Max his full attention, he said, "I would love to have chicken dumplings with you."

Rae thought it was sweet, the way he used Max's turn of phrase. And while Cole may not be the most enthusiastic person, she was beginning to see what a kind and caring soul he was. If only he'd smile more. Then again, that might make him downright irresistible.

No, stoic was better. Because there was no way she'd ever entrust her heart to another man.

Cole arrived at the Loving Hearts Nursing Home late the next afternoon, relieved that he no longer had to put Aunt Tilly off. It had taken him and Rae until almost eleven last night, but they'd made it through the binder and divvied up responsibilities, part of which included contacting each of the committee chairs to make sure they were on task with their duties.

Aside from that, there wasn't much for them to do until after Thanksgiving—a fact he found surprisingly disappointing. Now there was no reason for him to see Rae and the kids. That should make him happy. He was a loner, after all. So why was he looking for reasons to see them?

Because they'd breathed life into his stale existence.

He angled into a parking space and killed the engine. When Rae had told him that Max had asked about him, Cole had felt as though he suddenly had a purpose. That, maybe, he could make a difference in those kids' lives. And after what happened at the park yesterday, he believed he'd made some inroads in his relationship with little Max. But how could he build on that if he wasn't with the kid?

His phone buzzed in his pocket. He pulled it out, a twinge of something akin to excitement pulsing through him when he glimpsed Rae's name on the screen. Was Max asking to see him? Did he want Cole to join them at the park again?

Then he read the text.

M & M are refusing to go to the park. They're afraid those boys will be there.

Cole cringed. He hated that Max and Maggie had been bullied. The park should be a safe haven. A place to have fun. Now it had been marred by the actions of some boys whose lives had been impacted by the same insensitivity.

His thumbs moved over the screen.

I could meet you there.

He hit Send and waited.
A moment later, she responded.

They're saying they don't want to go. Appreciate the offer, though.

Shaking his head, he tucked his phone away. Without the park, Maggie and Max had nowhere to play. And that was just plain sad.

He retrieved a box of MoonPies from the passenger seat, recalling his exchange with the older boys yesterday. They'd seemed to think taunting and even hitting were just a part of life.

Exiting his truck, he thought about the angry outbursts his father used to have. To Cole's knowledge, the man had never hit Cole's mother. Still, Cole had lived in constant fear that he would.

He entered the nursing home, wondering what his life might have been like if his father had been as easygoing when Cole was growing up as he was now.

Moving beyond the inviting lobby, Cole made his way down the wide, carpeted hallway to the right. Doors lined each side, many of them open.

"Hi, Cole." Ida Brindle smiled and waved from her recliner in the first room on the right.

"Hey, Mrs. Ida." The gray-haired woman had been his Sunday school teacher when he was in second grade. To this day, his mouth still watered when he recalled her chocolate-chip cookies.

Mr. Jansen's television blared from the fourth door on the left. The man loved his game shows.

With a deep breath, Cole approached his father's room at the end of the hall. He rapped his knuckles against the door. "Hey, Leland." The man always seemed perplexed when Cole referred to him as Dad, so Cole had taken to calling him by his given name. "How's it going?"

His father looked up from his recliner. "Well, hello there, young man." His once dark hair was now white, though still just as thick. "What can I do for ya?"

"I just stopped by to give you these."

The man's eyes, a shade bluer than Cole's, lit up when Cole handed him the MoonPies. "How 'bout that? How'd you know these're my favorite?"

"Just a guess." The man could remember his favorite snack but not his own son.

"Well, thank ya kindly." At least this Leland was appreciative. He tore open the box and held it toward Cole. "Care for one?"

"No, I'm good."

"Pull up a chair. Tell me 'bout yourself." He removed the cellophane from the so-called pie that resembled a giant cookie while Cole perched on a side chair near the wall.

Resting his right ankle atop his left knee, Cole said, "Aw, I'd rather hear about you. You got any family, Leland?"

"Sure do. Prettiest wife south of the Red River. I'm not sure where she ran off to, but she should be back shortly." He took a bite of his chocolate-covered treat.

"Any kids?" Cole had no idea why he asked the same questions every time. Perhaps somewhere deep inside him he hoped his father might recognize him. But it would never happen. Leland lived in the past. A distorted one at that, where life was good and he adored his wife and son.

If only that were true.

"Oh, yes. He's a good-lookin' boy. Smart as a whip, too." The old man snapped his fingers. "Now I remember where Doris went."

Cole straightened. That was different. "Where's that?"

"She went to see some fella 'bout tuning our piano. That wife of mine knows how to tickle the ivories. She's been wantin' to teach our boy how to play."

Leland was correct that Cole's mother was a gifted piano player and that she'd wanted to teach Cole how to play. Yet, for all her attempts, he never had learned how to play. Anytime he'd tried to practice, his father would yell at him, saying he was making a bunch of racket.

The older man took another nibble of Moon-Pie, sending crumbs tumbling down the front of his chambray shirt and into his lap. "I sure wish you could hear her play."

So did Cole. The piano had been an escape for his mother. She'd close her eyes while her fingers moved up and down the keyboard, beckoning the most beautiful melodies from the piano that had belonged to her parents. It was the kind of music that could reach deep into your soul. It even had a calming effect on his father, the way David's harp playing soothed King Saul's torment.

"You'll have to come back 'round some other day. I know she'd be happy to play you a tune."

Cole stood, emotion tightening his throat. "I'll be sure and do that." He inched toward the door.

"Thank ya for stoppin' in, young man. What did you say your name was again?"

He hadn't. Just like every other time. At least, not until the old man asked at the end like he had just now. "Cole."

Leland's shaggy white brows lifted. "What a coincidence. That's my boy's name."

"You don't say?" Cole shoved his hands into his pockets. "Catch ya later, Leland." He hurried back up the hall, his long strides eating up the distance in half the time as his past warred with the present. He thought of all the verbal attacks he and his mother had endured. *God, why couldn't he have been like this when I was a kid?*

Returning to his truck, Cole fired it up and hastily made his way out of the parking lot. Yet instead of heading to his house in town, he found himself driving past the city limits to the house he'd grown up in. His mother had inherited the old farmhouse from her parents. After she passed, Cole had tried to give it to Tilly, but she hadn't wanted it any more than he had. That hadn't stopped her from hemming and hawing when he'd talked about selling it, though. And there was no way Cole could live there, surrounded by so many painful memories.

In the end, he'd decided to hang on to it until Tilly passed. He simply checked in on it every week or so to make sure everything was still in working order.

Now, as he pulled into the drive of the folk Victorian, he noticed that the pale yellow paint had begun to peel. He remembered when his mother chose the color, claiming it made her happy. If anyone had ever deserved a little happiness in her life, it had been Doris Heinsohn.

He parked toward the back and made his way onto the porch that spanned two-thirds of the backside of the house. After unlocking the door, he stepped into the modest kitchen with its faux-brick laminate floor, 1960's wood cabinets and wood-paneled walls, and reached for the light switch in an attempt to illuminate the dark, dreary space.

Continuing into the living room, he found himself drawn to the piano hugging the wall to his right. Dust covered the dark oak finish. He lifted the lid and pecked at a few keys. It needed to be tuned. But since there was no one to play it, that would have to be a job for the next owner.

He took in the rest of the room that was just

the way his mother had left it, right down to the home magazines on the Victorian-style coffee table. Someday he'd need to empty the place. But that would mean spending time here, going through every nook and cranny, and he didn't have the energy for that. Perhaps never would.

He returned to the kitchen, suddenly eager to escape. The wooden screen door creaked as he pushed it open. He sucked in a breath of fresh air and locked the door behind him.

As he approached the steps, he looked out over the expansive yard with its large live oaks and a pecan grove near the back. The land his father once ranched had been sold off, save for the five acres around the house. When Cole was a kid, this land had been his haven. An escape from his father's bullying.

Descending the trio of steps, he thought of Maggie and Max, and the bullies who had quelled their desire to go to the park today. The setting sun filtered through the trees as he continued into the yard. If only Maggie and Max had a safe haven like this. A place where they wouldn't have to worry about other kids.

You could build a play area for them.

Where had that thought come from?

While birds chattered overhead, he twisted left then right, taking in the large grassy area. There was plenty of space. Still…

Rae could even do her laundry while they played, instead of having to take them to the Laundromat.

Anxiety twisted in his gut. Where were all these crazy notions coming from? Not that they didn't have merit. Still, just because he had the means to do something so extravagant didn't mean he should. Then again, it would add value to the house whenever he was ready to sell.

Who would he get to build one of those big playsets, though? How long would it take?

Pulling his phone from his pocket, he scrolled through his contacts until he found Wes Bishop's number. His thumb hovered over the screen. While Wes was a local contractor, he was also Rae's brother. If Cole decided to proceed with this, he'd have to make sure Wes was willing to keep things under wraps because, if Rae found out, she might start asking questions.

He tapped the screen and Wes answered on the third ring. "Wes, Cole Heinsohn here. I have an idea I'd like to run past you."

"Sure, lay it on me."

Cole laid out his plans along with his reasoning. "Those kids have been traumatized enough. They shouldn't be afraid to play outside."

"I hear you on that, Cole. And all I can say

is that this must be a God thing, because the job I was supposed to start on Monday called not ten minutes ago to tell me they needed to postpone for a week."

"Could you tackle this project in only a week?"

"Don't see why not, depending on the scope of the work, of course. What are you thinking?"

Scrutinizing the large grassy area that had been taken over by weeds, he said, "A couple of swings, maybe one of those forts and a slide. No, make that two slides. A straight one and a winding one."

"You'll also need some sand or mulch for cushioning the area around it."

"Good thinking." If one of the kids were to fall, he wanted them to have a soft landing.

"Sounds simple enough," said Wes. "If you're available, we can meet tomorrow. Say, about this time. I can look at the space and we'll go over the different types of equipment."

"Great. I'll see you tomorrow then."

And in a little over a week, Maggie and Max would have their own personal playground.

He could hardly wait.

Chapter Five

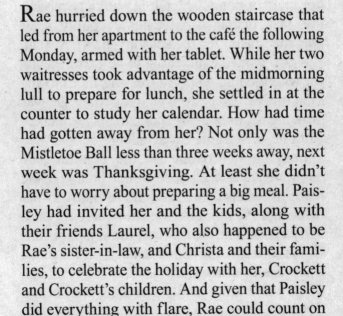

Rae hurried down the wooden staircase that led from her apartment to the café the following Monday, armed with her tablet. While her two waitresses took advantage of the midmorning lull to prepare for lunch, she settled in at the counter to study her calendar. How had time had gotten away from her? Not only was the Mistletoe Ball less than three weeks away, next week was Thanksgiving. At least she didn't have to worry about preparing a big meal. Paisley had invited her and the kids, along with their friends Laurel, who also happened to be Rae's sister-in-law, and Christa and their families, to celebrate the holiday with her, Crockett and Crockett's children. And given that Paisley did everything with flare, Rae could count on the day being a real treat for Max and Maggie.

Switching to the Notes app, she glanced over

her to-do list for the Mistletoe Ball, wishing she didn't see it as such an albatross. The ball was for a good cause. It benefitted kids like Max and Maggie, whose foster parents might not be able to afford the extra gifts. But having to oversee the whole thing weighed on her and occupied her mind, making it difficult to concentrate on her own holiday plans. And now that Paisley had decided to have her wedding the week before Christmas and asked Rae to be her maid of honor, she felt her anxiety mounting. That, of course, made her feel guilty. Jesus was the reason for the season; she knew that. But she wanted everything to be extra special for Maggie and Max by treating them to the kind of Christmas she'd enjoyed when she was growing up, back before her parents were taken from her in a tragic car accident.

Leaving her phone on the counter, she straightened and grabbed a shortbread cookie from the glass case. Just one of many sweet offerings Paisley provided for the café on a daily basis. As Rae savored the crisp, pecan-flavored treat, she thought back on all those Christmases when she was little. They'd been filled with traditions like choosing and cutting down the Christmas tree, baking cookies, decorating gingerbread houses, driving around to look at Christmas lights, attending Christmas concerts at school and church. How she longed for those days and wanted Maggie and Max to enjoy the same experiences. To have a Christmas they would always remember. That way, even if the adoption fell through, she could take heart in knowing that the kids would always have happy memories of their time together.

Her phone chimed, startling her from her thoughts. Seeing Tina Schmidt's name on the screen, Rae couldn't help wondering why she'd be calling. Sure, Tina was one of the committee chairs for the Mistletoe Ball, but she had the easiest job of all, considering the band had been booked since last year's ball.

Picking up the phone, she tapped the screen and pressed the phone to her ear. "Hi, Tina."

"Hey, Rae." A sigh came through the line. "I'm afraid I have some bad news."

Rae couldn't imagine what. Unless Tina had to vacate her position for some reason, leaving Rae in charge. Ha! At least this one would be easy.

"Go ahead."

"The band we booked for the ball has canceled. Or more to the point, they've disbanded."

"What?" Rae struggled to temper the angst rising in her core. "They can't do that. Don't these people know they have a contract to fulfill?"

"Yeah…um, we didn't do a contract. I mean, they're friends of ours and they're a family. I never imagined they'd break up the group."

Rae paced back and forth behind the counter, willing herself to remain calm. "I hope you have some other ideas then, Tina. The ball always has dancing, and people can't dance without a band."

"Technically, that's not true. You *can* dance without a band. You just can't dance without music."

Rae paused near the door to the kitchen. "Speakers and someone's playlist will not cut it, all right?"

"I know. I've already been thinking. My husband's brother's sister-in-law knows a guy who's in a band. She said she'd check with him."

Rae dropped her head into her hand. She didn't have time for this. Not when she had a perfect Christmas to plan. "Any idea what type of music they play?"

"No. I s'pose I should check on that."

"Most definitely." While people around Bliss appreciated a little polka now and then, they expected a cover band that performed pop and country music at the ball. "And the sooner, the better."

"All right. I'll call you back just as soon as I know something."

Ending the call, she stared at her phone. "Of all the crazy...why wouldn't you have a contract?"

"I don't know."

She whirled to find Cole standing at the far end of the counter, near the cash register, looking as handsome as ever in a charcoal pinstripe suit.

"But as an attorney, I'd recommend one."

Hand to her chest as though it would settle her erratic heartbeat, she moved toward him. Except for church yesterday, she'd barely seen him since the night they'd finished Tilly's binder. That was a week ago. She tried not to take it personally, choosing to believe that his absence had nothing to do with her or the kids and was only because he'd had to be in court twice last week. That was why she hadn't contacted him. Now that they each had their assignments, only a few of which overlapped— like setup and the silent auction—there was no need, except maybe to discuss ticket sales. All of the committee chairs were expected to sell tickets, including her and Cole. And as of the last report, sales were way up compared to last year.

"Sorry, I haven't been around much." He

strolled across the wood floor, meeting her halfway. "Wouldn't want you to feel like I've abandoned you." He paused beside one of the tables. "How are Maggie and Max?"

"They're fine. And no worries. You have clients to take care of." The last thing he needed to worry about was her and the kids, even though the kids asked about him anytime she mentioned the park. By Thursday, they'd finally gathered the courage to return, but only if Cole was there. And while that kind of bothered her, she couldn't say she blamed them, either. The way he'd come to their rescue with those bullies had been pretty spectacular. Still, she hadn't been able to bring herself to call him.

"My schedule is looking much calmer for the foreseeable future." He studied her intently. "Is something wrong?"

"I just got off the phone with Tina Schmidt. Seems our band for the ball has disbanded. And, as you heard, there was no contract."

"That's not good. What are we going to do?"

She lifted a shoulder. "Let Tina handle it. At least, for now. However, based on our conversation, I don't have high expectations."

His penetrating gaze remained fixed on her. "There's got to be something we can do."

"You mean besides sic Tilly on her?" A nervous laugh bubbled out. "That is, of course, unless you know someone who's in a band."

Studying the tin ceiling tiles, he shook his head. "No. However—" he looked at her now "—I have a client who's a DJ. He does a lot of weddings in the Austin area."

She hadn't considered a DJ. "That might work. *If* he's available the night of the ball. I mean, we're talking only three weeks out during the busiest time of year."

"Let me check with him." He pulled his phone from inside his jacket and moved his thumbs over the screen for a few moments before tucking it away again.

Nervous energy pulsed through her. Moving behind the counter, she grabbed her mug, ready for a refill. "Can I get you something? A coffee, perhaps?"

"No, I just came by to check in. I don't want you to feel like I'm shirking my duties."

Filling her cup with dark roast, she said, "So long as the committee chairs do what they're supposed to, I think we're okay."

He nodded. "You and the kids haven't had any more problems with those boys at the park, have you?"

"Actually, we haven't been to the park since that day."

Distress marred his handsome features. "Why not?"

She set her cup on the counter, wondering if she dared tell him it was because they wanted him to go with them? No. She'd come across as inept and needy, and she was neither of those things.

"What happened with those boys upset them. They'll come around, though."

"I hate to see them miss out just because of one bad experience."

"I know. It's sad."

He grew quiet, glancing toward the window before addressing her again. "Perhaps they'd feel more comfortable if I went with you. It's supposed to be a nice day."

She couldn't help noticing he didn't seem quite as enthusiastic as he had in the past. Was he simply taking pity on her? But then, if it would get the kids to the park so they could see things were all right, then maybe they'd be encouraged enough to go without him. "Possibly. I guess it wouldn't hurt to ask." Not that she didn't already know the answer.

"Please do." The intensity in his gaze made her mouth go dry.

"I will. As soon as they get home from school."

He smiled. "Good. Just let me know." A beep

sounded from his jacket. He pulled out his phone and looked at the screen. "Good news. My client says he's available the night of the ball. He also included a link to his web page."

"Awesome. Send it to me and I'll check it out."

"Done." A couple of taps later, he returned the phone to his pocket and gave her his full attention. "On second thought, give me a small dark roast, black, to go, and one of those pumpkin bars." He pointed to the case.

Rae filled the cup, added a lid and set it in front of him before slipping the dessert into a foam box. "Anything else?"

"Not right now." He retrieved his wallet and handed her a ten spot. As she was gathering his change, he asked, "What are your lunch specials today?"

Given that he rarely patronized the café except for the occasional visit with a client, his question took her by surprise. "Beef tips and cheese enchiladas."

"Tough choice."

She handed him his change. "I usually tell my customers to get both and save one for dinner."

"Sounds like good business sense to me." After tucking away his wallet, he grabbed his order and started for the door. "Let me know what the kids say about the park."

"Will do." She watched him exit the café and amble past the front window on the way back to his office, trying to ignore the thrill bubbling inside her. Cole's interest in the kids made him way too attractive. He was proving to be a good role model with his calm demeanor, though, showing the kids that not all men were like their father.

But he has no interest in you, she quickly reminded herself. If it wasn't for the Mistletoe Ball, Cole wouldn't be coming around at all. And that was fine by Rae. After what her cheating ex-husband had put her through, she had no interest in opening herself up to that kind of pain again.

No, her heart's desire was to be a mother. And she didn't need a man for that.

Cole pulled up to his parents' house Wednesday afternoon to see how the play area was coming. He was eager to see it completed. Then Maggie and Max would have a safe place to play without needing him there to protect them. Not that he didn't want to be there, but it was for the best.

Last week, he'd been too busy with work to spend any time with Rae and the kids, and he'd missed them terribly. Found himself thinking about them all the time, wondering if there'd been any more problems at the park. Countless times he'd reached for his phone, longing to call Rae. Yet he'd stopped himself. Longing wasn't a part of his vocabulary.

Dropping by the café on Monday had been a huge mistake. All it had done was remind him of how much he enjoyed Rae's company. Seemed the more he was with her and the kids, the more he wanted to be with them. The four of them had gone to the park the past two days and were slated to meet again in an hour. They'd invited him for dinner and he'd eagerly accepted.

He heaved a sigh, well aware he was stepping into dangerous territory. He was Leland Heinsohn's son, after all. That alone had been enough to keep him from building any sort of relationship for nearly fifty years. There was no reason to change now. So why was staying away from them such a struggle?

Because they made him feel alive. Gave him something to look forward to. But protecting them had to be his top priority. Even if it meant staying away. He could live with that. Couldn't he?

Once the play area was finished, he and Rae would have to maintain a working relationship for the Mistletoe Ball, but that wouldn't require them to spend a lot of time together. Then, once the ball was over, he wouldn't have to see her again except, perhaps, in passing, the way it had been before Tilly had brought them together.

Just thinking about walking away made him sad. But that was the way it had to be if he wanted Rae and the kids to remain safe.

The whirring sound of a drill met his ears as he stepped out of his truck.

Across the way, Wes looked up. "Hey, Cole." He waved from the base of the large cedar structure that now sported two slides.

A sad smile twisted Cole's mouth. Maggie and Max were going to love this. Too bad he wouldn't be able to see them enjoy it.

"Looks like things are coming along quite nicely." Approaching, he admired the shingled fort-type structure atop one of the slides.

"It's gettin' there. I'll finish hanging the swings and this rock-climbing wall tomorrow." Wes motioned to the wooden wall he was in the process of attaching colorful faux rocks to. "Then my crew and I will get the entire area mulched Friday morning and be out of your way."

Cole admired the craftsmanship. "You've done a great job here. The kids are really going to love this." Now they'd be free to play without looking over their shoulder. Though the older boys had yet to return to the park, Maggie and Max always seemed to keep a watchful eye. He prayed their counselor could help them overcome that, though he knew from personal experience it took time. Being exposed to good people, realizing not everyone angered easily, had helped him.

That was why he had to distance himself from Rae and the kids. While he'd never had any anger issues, he'd also chosen to live in a fairly controlled environment, keeping to himself and avoiding as many social events as possible. He'd rather people believe him aloof or reclusive than tempestuous.

His phone rang and he pulled it from the pocket of his slacks to see Tilly's name on the screen. "You'll have to excuse me, Wes."

"Not a problem."

Cole started in the direction of his truck as Wes returned to his work. "Hello, Tilly."

"Cole, I'm afraid we might have a problem."

As if he needed more problems. "Is it something to do with the ball?"

"Well, I'm not sure." She sighed. "It's Rae. I just got off the phone with her and…well, I'm worried she might be feeling a bit overwhelmed."

Between the café, the kids and having to oversee the Mistletoe Ball, it wouldn't surprise him. Rae had her hands full. "Did she say that?"

"No, but there was something in her tone. I can't quite put my finger on it, but she seemed distressed."

"I understand your concern, but I'm not sure how I can help." As an attorney, he was more of a straight shooter than the sympathetic type.

"You can sit down with her and talk face-to-face. See if there's something she might need assistance with."

His shoulders sagged as he leaned against the bumper of his truck. "Even if there was, I doubt she'd be comfortable opening up to me." Granted, they did seem to be forming something he supposed was friendship. Mostly because of the kids. Still, that's precisely what he was trying to avoid.

"Cole, you're an attorney. You have ways of getting people to talk."

In the courtroom, perhaps, but not in real life. He tried to avoid conversations that went beyond the boundaries of superficial. Because then he risked becoming invested.

He looked back at the play area, realizing he was already invested. In the kids, anyway. He simply wanted to make things easier for their beautiful foster mom.

"I don't know, Tilly." His gaze lifted to a cardinal perched on the limb of a live oak. "Rae is pretty independent."

"That's exactly my point! She's not the type to ask for help, so we need to pry it out of her."

We meaning him.

He shoved a hand through his hair, wishing he didn't have such a soft spot for his mother's sister. "All right, I'll see what I can do." At least it would give them something to talk about while the kids played today.

"Oh, you're such a sweet boy."

Pushing away from the pickup, he shook his head. "I'm not making any promises, though. It's not like she'll be under oath or anything. If she doesn't want to open up, I can't make her."

"You'll do fine, dear. Keep me posted."

"Yes, ma'am." Ending the call, he shoved the phone back into his pocket and kicked at a clump of dirt. So much for trying to distance himself. If Rae were to share her troubles with him, that would only make him want to help all the more.

He rejoined Wes as the last yellow rock was screwed into place.

Wes straightened, taking in the playset. "I gotta say, I'm impressed you're willing to do this for Rae and the kids. I mean, these things aren't cheap."

Lifting a shoulder, Cole said, "It's only money. What better way to use it than to bring smiles to the faces of two little kids?"

Rae's brother looked at him. "Are you sure this is just about the kids?"

"Positive."

Wes held up his hands. "I was just checking. Rae is my sister, after all. Still, it's good to see someone do something nice for her. After what her ex put her through…"

While Cole had heard Rae was divorced, he had no idea about the circumstances. Judging by Wes's remark, though, Rae had gotten hurt.

Still, it wasn't any of Cole's business. He and Rae were little more than acquaintances. They both had pasts. Things neither of them cared to share.

So why was Wes's comment chewing a hole in Cole's stomach?

Chapter Six

She was the worst mother ever.

Rae sat at a picnic table in the shade of an oak tree at the park, watching Maggie and Max take turns on the slide. After receiving a call from Maggie's teacher telling her what Maggie had done, they shouldn't be here at all. Further proof of what a bad parent she was.

If only Maggie would talk to her. Explain why she'd done something so out of character. Instead, the girl had clammed up when Rae confronted her.

"Sorry I'm late."

Turning, she saw Cole approach, hands buried in the pockets of his charcoal slacks, the collar of his pale gray button-down loosened. Did the man have any idea how good looking he was?

She glanced at her watch. "I hadn't even

noticed." Looking up at him, she continued. "Even if I had, it's no big deal. You have meetings and other important things to tend to."

"Mr. Cole!" Max waved from the bottom of the larger slide. "Watch me."

The man did just that, a hint of a smile erupting as the boy whizzed down the apparatus. "You're a pro!" he hollered.

"Hi, Mr. Cole." Maggie waved as she climbed the ladder for another go.

He waved back before giving Rae his full attention.

Suddenly uneasy under his scrutiny, she said, "You may as well go hang out with them. I'm afraid I'm not very good company today."

"And why is that?" He eased beside her on the bench without blocking her view of the kids. "Are there more issues with the ball? If so, just let me know and I'll take care of them."

"If only it were that simple."

"You mean like subbing the DJ for the band?"

"Yeah." As soon as Tina had notified them her lead on a band was a dead end, they'd booked Cole's client.

He leaned closer, his shoulder bumping hers. "I can tell something's bothering you. And while I'm more than happy to listen and help any way I can, I also understand if you don't want to talk about it."

Frustration had her heaving a sigh. She was not a needy person. She was used to facing challenges on her own. So why did she find herself wanting to open up to Cole? Maybe because he was an attorney, someone who knew how to keep confidences. Or perhaps it was because she'd seen how much he cared for Maggie and Max.

Pushing up the sleeves of her Henley, she studied the puffy clouds drifting aimlessly overhead. "I received a call from Maggie's teacher today. Seems my sweet little girl excused herself to go to the restroom, but when she failed to come back in a reasonable amount of time, her teacher went looking for her."

"Where was she?"

Rae could hear the concern in his voice. "Oh, she was in the restroom, all right." She looked at him now. "Painting the walls and mirrors with the teacher's nail polish."

While his mouth dropped open, she saw the corners twitching.

"This is no laughing matter, Cole. We're talking theft and vandalism."

He cleared his throat, his expression turning serious. "I think the bigger question here is why she did it."

"I've been trying to figure that out."

"Have you spoken with her?"

"Yes." Not that it did any good. "They dismissed her for the rest of the day, so we had a little one-on-one."

"And?"

She watched the kids run from the slide to the swings, Maggie laughing as if nothing had happened. "When I asked her why she did it, all I got was a shoulder shrug and a pitiful 'I don't know.'" Resting her elbow on the table, she dropped her chin in her hand. "This is all my fault."

"Given all Maggie has been through, I doubt that."

"I don't. I've been so focused on Max and his issues that I failed to recognize Maggie was dealing with her own stuff."

"You're being awful hard on yourself."

From where Rae sat, she deserved it. "Don't you see? Maggie was entrusted to me and I failed her. And if I can't find that Country Girl doll she wants for Christmas, I'll fail her again." She dropped her forehead against the tabletop, feeling more than a little sorry for herself. That made her feel even worse because it was Maggie she should be focusing on, not herself.

"Come on, Rae." He touched her shoulder, coaxing her to sit up. "Christmas is the last thing you need to be worrying about. It's still five weeks away."

"Are you kidding?" Straightening, she glowered at him. "I've been shopping online for weeks." Her angst ratcheted up a notch with each sentence. "Stuff is selling out already. Like Maggie's doll."

Looking as calm as ever, Cole simply stared at her. "Any idea when they'll get more?"

"January."

"Oh." He shifted uncomfortably. "At least you've got time to find it somewhere else. Just because it's sold out online doesn't mean they won't have it in stores."

A car honked as it passed, and she instinctively waved even though she didn't have a clue who was driving.

"I don't have time to go to the city. At least, not until after the ball. Even then, I'd have to take the kids. I can't shop for them when they're with me. That's why I've been doing as much as I can online." She blew out an exasperated breath that puffed her cheeks. "I should have ordered the doll when she first mentioned it."

He continued to watch her. "Where are you hiding all these gifts?"

"In one of the pantries in the café. The kids aren't allowed in the kitchen, so they should remain undiscovered. Even if they do get in there, the gifts are in plain cardboard boxes, on the top shelves."

"You are a wise woman."

"Who was once a kid who liked to snoop."

"Back to the shopping." He cocked his head. "Someone could babysit the kids."

"True. But Wes and Laurel are the only people the kids are comfortable with and I hate relying on them all the time."

"I could watch them. That is, if you're okay with that. The kids know me, and I *think* they like me. We'd have fun."

Great, now he was feeling sorry for her. "I appreciate that, Cole, I really do."

"But?"

She watched the kids scurry back and forth, their happy chatter filling the air. "What if I still can't find it?"

"Come on, Maggie is not a demanding child. She'll appreciate anything she gets."

"That brings us right back to what happened today." Straightening, she gripped the edge of her seat. "I don't want her to feel like she's playing second fiddle. I want her to have something special. I want this Christmas to be perfect."

He lifted a brow. "To my knowledge, the perfect Christmas has only happened once, a few thousand years ago, and it was very modest. Except for the angels."

Another time she might have laughed. Instead, his comment only irritated her. "You know what I mean. I want to create as many happy memories for those two as I possibly can."

"I understand, but how much do you remember from Christmases when you were a kid?"

Her thoughts drifted back to the modest two-story Cape Cod in Arkansas, where she and Wes had grown up. "I remember searching for the perfect Christmas tree, caroling with friends, all the sweet treats my mom only made at Christmas. And, of course, all the decorations, the twinkling lights, the smell of cinnamon and cloves, Christmas music, gathering with family. I miss that."

"Where are your parents now?"

"They passed away when I was nineteen. Car accident. Christmases have never been the same since."

The lines in his brow deepened. "I'm sorry, Rae. That had to have been rough."

"It was harder on Wes." She shrugged. "He was only sixteen."

"Still in high school."

She nodded. "I put college on hold till he graduated and joined the Navy. School could wait. He needed me more."

Cole studied her for a long moment. So long,

it had her squirming. "You know, there aren't a lot of nineteen-year-olds who would have paused their lives like that."

"I don't think I could have lived with myself if I hadn't. Our grandparents had already passed and there was no way Wes would've survived with Aunt Veronica, our mom's sister, so it wasn't that tough of a decision."

"Perhaps. But it says a lot about who you are as a person."

Eager to deflect the attention away from herself, she looked at him. "What about you? What sort of Christmas memories do you have?"

Pain shadowed his features, his expression turning almost dark. "Christmas was very low-key at my house. My dad didn't care for a lot of fuss."

"Come on, you must have *some* fond memories."

He watched the kids rock back and forth on the horse and dinosaur spring riders. "Not really. The tree went up a few days before Christmas, came down the day after. Presents were opened Christmas morning and were usually all mine." He lifted a shoulder. "Occasionally we'd go to Tilly's on Christmas Eve or for Christmas dinner, but that was the exception, not the rule."

Watching him, Rae couldn't help but feel as

though she was missing something. He looked so sad. She couldn't imagine not having *some* happy memories of Christmases past. Only part of the reason she was determined to make things special for Maggie and Max.

"Mr. Cole!"

He looked in Max's direction. "What's up, buddy?"

"Wanna come help me slide?"

"Are you kidding?" Cole's countenance brightened as he pushed to his feet. "I live to help you." He winked at Rae. "Duty calls."

She shook her head as he walked away. Maggie and Max weren't Cole's duty. Yet he had embraced them. Gone out of his way to make sure Max didn't see him as a threat. But the sorrow she'd seen when he'd spoken about his Christmases as a child tugged at her heart and made her want to include him in her holiday plans. To prove to him that Christmas really was the most wonderful time of the year.

Cole's resolve to stay away from Rae and the kids was crumbling fast. Especially after talking with her at the park Wednesday. She was a wonderful mother to Maggie and Max. Didn't she realize that every parent felt like a failure at some point?

Nonetheless, he'd tried to help her out the

past couple of nights, offering to play with Max so she and Maggie could have a little time to themselves. To his knowledge, though, Maggie wasn't offering up any answers for her delinquent behavior. At least she was getting attention. That could have been why she'd acted out. Lots of kids did bad things simply for the attention.

He glanced in his rearview mirror on Friday afternoon to see Rae's SUV following him. Wes had completed work on the play area this morning and after checking things out on his lunch break, Cole couldn't wait to show it to Rae and the kids. Maggie and Max were going to be so excited.

A few minutes later, he pulled into the drive at his folks' place and parked beside the farmhouse, closer to the front instead of following the drive around back as he usually did. He wanted to be with the kids and to see the looks on their faces when they saw his surprise.

"What a lovely old home," Rae said as she exited her vehicle.

"This is where I grew up." He walked to the passenger side of the SUV to help Maggie out. The temperature was perfect this afternoon. Not too hot, not too cool. A great day to be outside.

"Does anyone live here?" Rae looked from the house to him.

"No. It's been empty since my mom passed a few years ago. My dad is at Loving Hearts Nursing Home."

She paused beside Max's door. "I don't understand. Why are we here then?"

"Because I have something I want to show you." The skepticism on her face had trepidation infringing on his excitement. What if Rae didn't like his idea or found it inconvenient? Perhaps he should have discussed the play area with her before forging ahead.

Without opening Maggie's door, he motioned for Rae to join him at the back of her vehicle. Lowering his voice, he said, "After the incident with those boys at the park, I kept thinking how nice it would be if you had a backyard. A safe place where Maggie and Max were free to enjoy themselves without worrying about other kids." He eyed the sweeping front porch. "This house not only has a big backyard, but five acres just waiting to be explored. So I contacted your brother and asked him to help me with a little project."

One eyebrow lifted and her gaze narrowed. "What sort of project?"

He sucked in a breath. "Grab the kids and I'll show you."

Soon, Maggie and Max were skipping alongside him as they continued around the side of the house. Under the shade of an old live oak, Maggie peered up at him. "What do you want to show us, Mr. Cole?"

When they'd reached the corner of the house, he motioned toward the once forsaken space that now boasted a sprawling wood fort with tire swings, a rock-climbing wall, two slides, monkey bars, regular swings and a host of other accessories, and said, "This!"

"Whoa!" Maggie's and Max's mouths both fell open.

"Oh, my—" Rae pulled up short to Maggie's right. "Cole Heinsohn, what have you done?"

"Given the kids a pretty awesome play space, I hope."

"Can we go play?" Max tugged on Cole's arm.

He deferred to the woman next to him. "Rae?"

"Go ahead." As the kids took off running, she glared at Cole. "That had to have cost a ton of money."

"Maggie and Max are worth it." He couldn't help smiling, watching them beeline for the rock-climbing wall. "They deserve to be happy. To have a place where they're free to be kids." Tearing his gaze away from the delighted children, he looked down at her. "And their foster mom doesn't have to worry about others infringing on their fun."

Her rigid shoulders relaxed a notch.

"Follow me." He led her onto the large back porch and unlocked the back door before handing her the key. "I'm giving this to you. Feel free to come in here anytime and make yourself at home."

"Cole, I can't—"

"Yes, you can." He pushed the door open and stepped into the kitchen. "It's not fancy, but everything is functional. At least, I think so. I maintain the house, but no one has lived here for three years. You can bring your laundry and do it while the kids play. Laundry room is right there." He pointed to the open door to their left. "If you need to work on something, you can do it here at the table, where you can watch them play." He gestured to the window beside the door. "If you want to cook, you can do that. Whatever you like."

She shook her head. "I can't believe you would do this."

"Why? Because you think I'm an ogre or something?"

Her gaze shot to his. "I do not think you're an ogre. It's just…" Her gaze traversed the space. "This is a nice house. Why don't you live here?"

"It's too big for one person." Not to mention all the unpleasant memories it held. "It belonged to my mother's parents. She inherited it from them."

Rae wandered into the living room, rubbing her arms as she went. "It's really nice. A little dated, but that's easily remedied." She turned a skeptical gaze toward him. "Have you considered renting it out?"

"Why?" He waited in the opening between the kitchen and living room. "Are you interested?"

"No, I'd best stick to my apartment over the café for the time being." She peered down the hallway.

"And I'm not all that interested in becoming a landlord, so there you go."

Arms now crossed, she said, "You can hire people to do that for you, you know."

He shrugged. "Not interested."

Moving around the floral sofa to the piano, her gaze darted around the room. "Yet you're willing to dump a load of money on a backyard playground."

"If it'll bring smiles to the faces of three very special people, yes. Besides, if I ever do decide to let this place go, the backyard will be a huge selling point."

Suddenly, Rae began blinking rapidly and

promptly turned her back to him. "I don't know what to say, Cole."

He hadn't anticipated her becoming emotional and wasn't sure how he felt about that. Mostly because it made him want to take her in his arms and tell her he'd do anything to protect her and the kids. Instead, he cleared his throat and said, "'Thank you' will suffice."

After a moment, she squared her shoulders and faced him again, though tears still shimmered in her blue eyes. "Thank you, Cole."

His phone rang, granting him a reprieve from the intensity of the moment. Pulling it from his pocket, he looked at the screen. "It's the nursing home. Excuse me."

He hurried through the kitchen, out the door and onto the porch, where the sound of children's laughter filled the sweet-smelling air. "Hello?"

"Mr. Heinsohn, this is Sandra from Loving Hearts. There's been an incident with your father that requires your attention."

Cole's muscles tensed. "What happened?"

"One of the workers went into Leland's room and found him standing. Before she could get to him, he lost his balance and fell, hitting his arm on the bedside table."

Cole pinched the bridge of his nose. Leland falling wasn't an uncommon occurrence. Just like he didn't remember Cole, he often forgot he couldn't walk. He'd never injured himself, though.

"There's a pretty big gash on his right arm that's going to need stitches."

"I'll be right there." Heart racing, he ended the call. "I have to go." He eyed Rae as she emerged from the house.

Concern creased her brow. "Is something wrong?"

"My father fell." He started down the steps. "Sounds like I'm going to have to take him to the ER."

"Oh, no." She followed him. "Is there anything I can do?"

"No. You just see to it that Maggie and Max have fun." He waved to the kids. "You've got the keys. Stay as long as you like and lock up when you leave."

He jogged to the front of the house and threw himself into his truck. This was the third time his father had fallen in the past two months.

Cole started the engine and aimed his pickup toward town, praying the injury wasn't too bad. No, they would have called an ambulance if that had been the case.

He released a long, slow breath, trying to compose himself. At least the nurse's call had given him a reason to leave. He'd never imagined Rae would get so teary-eyed. Yes, his departure had been for the best. Rae and the kids wouldn't need him anymore. And he wouldn't worry. They'd be safe. Just the way he'd planned.

There was one thing he hadn't counted on, though—the giant hole their absence would leave on his heart.

Chapter Seven

Rae paced the wooden floorboards of the covered back porch at Cole's parents' house late the next afternoon, waiting for him to arrive. To say that she was taken aback by Cole's generous gesture was the understatement of the century. Downright flabbergasted was more like it. People didn't spend thousands of dollars on a backyard playset for somebody else's children. Especially when said children were still considered temporary.

Cole barely knew Maggie and Max, so Rae couldn't help thinking she was missing some very important pieces of the puzzle. Why did he seem so invested in her foster kids?

That was today's million-dollar question. One she was determined to find the answer to, no matter how busy he claimed he was.

Pausing, she leaned against the wood railing to watch Maggie and Max chase each other around the tree-filled yard, their giggles carrying on a gentle breeze. Despite Thanksgiving being only five days away, temperatures were in the mid-seventies. The sun filtered through the leaves of a large oak to dapple the ground with light. They were having so much fun.

Her gaze moved beyond the play area, scanning several acres dotted with majestic trees. This must have been an amazing place to grow up. So much wide-open space.

Yanking her attention back to the massive wooden structure that sported more equipment than the park, she wondered what had compelled Cole to do such a thing. And what did he want in return?

The sound of gravel crunching under tires drew her attention to the driveway as Cole's truck eased to a stop. Seconds later, he emerged, wearing a black T-shirt over faded jeans and worn boots.

Approaching the bottom step, he peered up at her. "What's the problem?"

She had to force herself to look away as her mind contemplated which version of Cole she liked best, the well-attired attorney or the hunky average Joe.

"Problem?" she finally managed to squeak out.

"When you called, you said there was a problem here at the house."

Snap out of it, Rae. You've seen good-looking men before.

"Mr. Cole!" the kids yelled in unison.

Turning, he shielded his eyes from the sun until he spotted them waving from the fort. "Looks like you two are having a good time."

"Watch this!" Max ducked toward the slide. "Are you watching?"

"I sure am." The corners of Cole's mouth lifted as Max propelled himself down the winding slide. "Good job, Max."

"Come see, Mr. Cole." Maggie motioned for him to join them.

He shifted his attention to Rae.

"Go ahead. They won't be satisfied until they've showed you everything." She remained on the porch, watching as the kids walked him around the play area. He was so attentive and patient.

After they demonstrated the rock-climbing wall, Cole excused himself and rejoined her on the porch.

"How's your father?" She eased toward two rocking chairs with peeling white paint. "Was he hurt very badly?"

"A skin tear on his arm. They fixed him up, though." He paused. "Are you going to tell me what this problem is that you need me to address?"

"Yes." She settled into one of the chairs, motioning toward the other. "Have a seat."

He hesitated, shifting from one booted foot to the other. "I just assumed something was wrong inside the house."

"No."

Hands slung low on his hips, he looked somewhat agitated. "Then what's the problem?"

She pointed to the play area. "I want to know why you did that."

"I told you—"

"I know what you told me. I just think there's more to it. People don't drop thousands of dollars on something as extravagant as that when they don't have any kids." Her gaze bore into him now. "What are you not telling me, Cole? Why are you so taken with Maggie and Max?"

He remained silent for a long while, watching the kids play. What was he keeping from her? Why was he struggling to tell her the truth?

Dropping into the opposite chair, he said, "They've been through a lot in their short lives."

"Yes, they have."

He set the rocker into motion. "I feel for them. That's all."

She shook her head. "Sorry, I'm not letting you off that easy. There's more to it."

Looking everywhere but at her, he said, "I…" He worried his lip. "I can empathize with them."

That didn't make sense. "And how would you be able to do that?"

Finally, he looked at her and she saw the torment in his eyes as they morphed to a stormy gray. "Because I grew up in an abusive home."

Her shock must have showed because he quickly looked away. "It's not common knowledge, so I'd appreciate it if you'd keep it to yourself."

"Yes, of…of course." Now she felt terrible for pressing him. But she never would've imagined… "I'm so sorry, Cole." She touched his arm, but he jerked away and glared at her.

"I don't want your pity, Rae. That's exactly why I didn't tell you or anyone else."

"Well, excuse me for caring." The words came out harsher than she'd intended. She leaned back, crossed her arms and set the chair into a frenzied pace.

Silence fell between them for several minutes. She wasn't sure what she hated more—that she'd pressed him to reveal something so painful or that he mistook caring for pity. Either way, she never imagined he'd tell her something so…heart-wrenching.

Finally, he said, "I guess I can see where you'd be skeptical. Thinking I might have ulterior motives. And perhaps it was selfish of me. But I was telling the truth when I said I wanted them to have a place where they'd feel safe. I know what it's like to spend your life walking on eggshells, looking over your shoulder."

Fisting her hands in her lap to keep herself from reaching out to him, she watched him, wishing she could take away his pain. "Who hurt you, Cole?"

He stared straight ahead, his knuckles white as he gripped the arms of the chair, his Adam's apple bobbing. "My father. The abuse was verbal, psychological. And my mother was the main target."

"Words can be just as hurtful as a fist."

"Tell me about it. The way my mother would flinch sometimes, it was as though he'd struck her." He paused, dragging a hand over his suddenly weary face. "I always feared my father would hit her one day. It was our dirty little secret we kept hidden from the entire town. Something that's not easy in a place as small as Bliss."

"That's a lot to ask of a kid."

He nodded. "The ironic thing is my father

doesn't remember any of it. He has dementia. And to hear him talk about his wife and son, you'd think we were the all-American family."

She found herself wincing. "That's got to be tough."

"It is." He puffed out a sardonic laugh. "He's actually a nice guy now." Leaning forward, he clasped his hands and rested his elbows on his knees as he focused on the kids. "Unlike Maggie and Max, I was blessed to have some good male role models in my life while I was growing up. And that's what I'd hoped to be for Maggie and Max. I want them to know that not all men are mean or angry."

"I think you've done just that, Cole. Max wouldn't have warmed up to you otherwise."

"They're great kids, Rae." He looked her way. "You are an extraordinary woman to take on the role you have."

"They needed love and I happen to have plenty to give."

"They're blessed to have you."

A breeze stirred up a pile of dead leaves at the base of the steps, sending them tumbling end over end into the grass.

Since Cole had opened up to her about something so deeply personal, she felt it only fair she reciprocate. "I haven't told many people this, but I'm hoping to make their time with me permanent."

"You mean you want to adopt them?"

She nodded. "Once their father is convicted, his parental rights will be terminated. And so long as there are no other relatives willing to take them…"

Her phone buzzed in her pocket. She pulled it out and checked the screen to see her friend Christa's name. "Give me one second." She tapped the screen. "Hey, Christa."

"Thought you and the kids might be looking for something to do and wondered if you'd like to come see the puppies." Christa's golden retriever, Dixie, had delivered three weeks ago, but Rae had wanted to give the pups a little time to grow before introducing them to the kids. "All of them have opened their eyes now, so they are busier than ever."

"Oh, I have no doubt the kids would love that. Can you give me an hour?"

"Sure. We're not going anywhere."

Ending the call, Rae looked at Cole, hating to leave so abruptly when he'd just bared his soul to her. "How would you like to join me and the kids on an adventure?"

He eyed her suspiciously. "What sort of adventure?"

"You know Mick Ashford, right?"

"Sure. We went to school together and, more recently, I represented him in the custody case Sadie's grandparents had filed."

"Oh, yeah, that's right." After the deaths of Mick's sister and brother-in-law, Mick became his niece's guardian. In the end, the court sided with Mick.

"Well, he and Christa's dog had puppies—*thirteen* of them—and I promised the kids I'd take them to see them once their eyes were open. Today is that day."

"Thirteen puppies?" He looked from her to the kids and smiled. "They're going to love that."

"Why don't you come with us?"

"Christa invited you. I wouldn't feel right."

"She won't mind. And besides, I'm pretty sure this is going to be something you'd rather witness for yourself instead of listening to me tell you about it later."

"Maggie and Max and thirteen puppies. That will be quite a sight."

"Come on." She stood, tucking her phone away. "Help me round them up and we'll be on our way."

Cole stared out the window of Rae's SUV as they cruised through town and into the countryside, still trying to figure out why he'd told her about his father. He'd never revealed anything about his past to anyone. On the contrary, he'd kept it hidden in the darkest corners of his mind, praying the truth he tried so hard to hide would never come to light.

Until Rae confronted him.

Except it wasn't just her prodding that had him divulging the secret he'd lived with his entire life. He understood her wariness. Yet, for reasons he couldn't understand, he'd wanted to tell her. Something he still couldn't comprehend. Was it that he wanted her to know he could relate to Maggie and Max on another level, or had his burden become too much to bear?

Whatever the case, the intensity of their earlier conversation had him eager for something more lighthearted. And what could be a better distraction than puppies?

Several miles outside of town, the kids chattered in the back seat as Rae eased her SUV into the drive of a white, two-story farmhouse with a sprawling front porch and green trim.

"Yay! We're here!" Maggie cheered from behind Cole.

"I can't wait to see the puppies." Max's voice inched up an octave with each word.

After parking, Rae unhooked her seat belt and twisted to face the kids. "I want you to be very careful with the puppies. They're still tiny, so no picking them up unless an adult says it's okay. Then you need to be sitting down when you hold them, because they're going to be really squirmy—" smiling, she wrinkled her nose "—and they could wiggle right out of your hands. Okay?"

"Yes, ma'am," they said in unison.

"Look!" Maggie pointed toward the front of the vehicle. "There's Sadie."

Glancing his way, Rae said, "Maggie and Sadie are in the same class at school."

He watched the girl and Christa as they approached, pleased to know that Maggie had made at least one friend.

While Rae unbuckled Max, Cole opened Maggie's door, his gaze drifting to the cattle grazing in the pasture behind the house. His father had been a rancher, just like Mick's dad. But unlike Mr. Ashford, who'd passed his knowledge on to Mick, Leland hadn't had the patience to teach Cole. Just as well, he supposed. Ranching kept his father away from the house most days, giving his mother a reprieve from his torment.

"Hey there, Cole." Christa nodded in his direction as he closed the door.

"Hope you don't mind a tagalong," he said as he moved in front of the vehicle.

"Of course not. With thirteen puppies, we have plenty to go around." Her attention shifted to the kids. "Are you two ready to see the puppies?"

"Yes!" they cheered.

"Mama Rae says we have to be careful." Max was obviously taking this activity quite seriously.

Christa smiled. "Your mama Rae is such a smart woman." She led them to the back of the house and onto the covered porch. Reaching for the door, she said, "Mick has them corralled in the dining room with their mama."

"How is she faring?" Rae motioned for the kids to follow her friend inside.

"You know Dixie," Christa said over her shoulder. "She's taking everything in stride."

They continued through the mudroom and farmhouse kitchen before stopping at the opening to the combined living/dining room where the table and chairs had been moved out of the way to make space for a round pen about six feet in diameter constructed of wire panels.

"Hey, guys." Mick approached from the opposite side of the enclosure, surprise lighting his face when he spotted Cole. "Hey, buddy." He extended a hand and Cole took hold. "How's it going?"

"It's going well." Cole glanced toward the

cluster of squirming fur balls on the floor. "Looks like you've got your hands full."

"That's an understatement. When we decided to breed Dixie, we were thinking maybe six or seven puppies tops. But this…" Mick shook his head. "Too bad my cattle aren't this prolific."

"Why don't you kids sit down on the floor," said Christa, "and I'll hand each of you a puppy."

Without hesitation, the three kids complied. Then, one by one, she handed them each a puppy.

"Don't forget me," said Rae.

"Patience, my friend." Christa handed her one with a slightly darker coat. "Here you go."

Cole turned to see Mick handing him a puppy. "Oh. Okay." He enveloped the tiny, pale blond bundle in his hand as it whimpered. "You're all right." He held it closer. "I've got you, little one."

Max's laughter drew Cole's attention to the floor where the boy's pup licked him relentlessly.

"You are so cute." Beside Cole, Rae buried her nose in her little bundle.

Cole looked down at the package in his own arms to see dark brown eyes staring up at him. The whining had stopped, and his puppy looked at him as if Cole were his best friend in the whole world. Just like—

He abruptly handed the pup back to Mick. "You'll have to excuse me." With that, he turned on his heel and fled through the kitchen and mudroom until he was safely outside. He descended the porch steps, sucking in copious amounts of air, trying to quell myriad emotions ricocheting through his body. He shouldn't have come with Rae. Yet he'd never imagined—

He dragged a hand through his hair. He'd only wanted to see the kids enjoying the puppies, not realizing the memories the scene would unearth.

With the sun hanging over the western horizon, he picked up his pace, moving past Rae's SUV, across the cattle guard and up the drive, as if he could outrun the shadows of his past. Gravel crunched beneath each determined step.

"Cole! Wait up!" Rae's voice had him cringing. He didn't want her to see him like this. Especially not now. Wasn't it enough that he'd told her about his father?

Still, his steps slowed and, in moments, she was beside him.

"Are you okay?" Out of breath, she gulped for air. "What happened in there?"

He kept moving. Until her fingers wrapped around his wrist.

"Cole, please talk to me."

He stared into blue eyes that were brimming with questions.

Tell her.

He balled his fists at his sides. *I can't.*

She already knows your secret.

Focusing on a cow nursing its calf in the pasture, he said, "Earlier this week, you asked me if I had any happy Christmas memories. There is one."

"Tell me. Please?"

He rested his hands on his hips and continued to stare off in the distance. "My parents gifted me with a golden retriever puppy when I was seven. Bo became my constant companion, my closest confidant. In many ways, he was what we'd now call an emotional support animal. I told him all of my secrets and he never judged. He'd just snuggle closer and lick my face."

He lowered his head, his insides twisting as he pressed on. "But when I was nine, I did something that upset my father. I think I'd forgotten to do some chore. Strange, I can't even remember what it was. All I remember is my punishment."

"Which was?"

"He took Bo and gave him to somebody else."

"Oh, Cole."

His eyes stung, yet the words continued to spill out. "I felt as though my heart had been ripped out. Bo had been my best friend, and suddenly, he was gone. And it was my fault." He sniffed. "I remember pleading with my dad not to take him. Mom did, too. But he put the dog in his truck and when he came back, he was alone." His fists balled at his sides. "I was so angry with him."

He startled when Rae wrapped her arms around his waist. But instead of pulling away, he melted into her embrace, craving the comfort she so willingly offered.

"I'm so afraid I'll end up like him." The words were muffled against her sweet-smelling hair.

Breaking the connection, she glared up at him. "How could you even think such a thing? Cole, you're a good, kind man who won over the heart of a frightened little boy."

Looking into her eyes, he found himself wishing he could win her heart.

But Rae knew too much. He couldn't allow himself to think of her as anything but a friend. Because, just like Bo, Rae could be gone one day, too. Especially now that she knew the truth about his past.

No, he and Rae had been brought together

for the sole purpose of the Mistletoe Ball. And Cole would do well to remember that, lest he allow his heart to be broken again.

Chapter Eight

Thanksgiving was only four days away so, ready or not, the holiday season had arrived. And much to Rae's chagrin, she was definitely *not* ready. With Maggie and Max out of school this week and the Mistletoe Ball on tap for the following week, she had no idea when she'd find time to make a shopping trip to the city. Though she had no doubt it would be so far into the season that she'd have no chance of finding the doll Maggie wanted.

In the laundry room of Cole's parents' farmhouse, Rae sighed and folded another load while the kids slid, swung and climbed pretend mountains outside. Ever since the nail polish incident, she'd been uncertain how to proceed with Maggie. She wanted the girl to know her actions were inappropriate, but at the same time Rae didn't want to keep reminding Maggie she'd made a mistake. That left Rae in a quandary. If she wasn't able to get her hands on the one gift Maggie had asked for, would Maggie perceive that as part of her punishment? The thought broke Rae's heart.

The smack of the screen door in the kitchen had her abandoning her laundry. Beside the round wooden table, Maggie and Max breathed heavily as they peeled off their jackets, their cheeks rosy. Today's temps were a little on the chilly side, thanks to a front that had moved through overnight. Still, the kids had insisted they'd wanted to play. Rae supposed she couldn't blame them. The space Cole had had her brother—who'd never said a word—create in the backyard was pretty fantastic.

Thoughts of the man who'd bared his soul to her yesterday settled in her mind. She couldn't even begin to fathom what Cole's childhood must have been like and hated that she'd caused him to relive some painful memories. But how could he even begin to believe he'd become like his father?

"Can we have a snack?" Maggie's words tugged Rae back to the present.

"Sure thing." She grabbed the backpack, unzipped the top, pulled out two small water bottles and set them on the table. "We've got animal crackers, string cheese, raisins, granola bars and bananas."

"Cheese, please." Max grinned at his little rhyme.

"Me, too," said Maggie.

She settled the kids at the table and pulled out the snacks, along with a couple of coloring books and a giant box of crayons. "I need to finish folding laundry—" she pointed to the room off of the kitchen "—so just holler if you need me."

Returning to what seemed like a mountain of socks, Rae set to work pairing them while thoughts of Cole again played across her mind. He'd looked so sad at church this morning. And when she'd asked if he'd like to join them for lunch, he'd declined. Was he afraid she'd question him further? Or perhaps he was still dealing with the anguish of yesterday.

How difficult it must be for him to have to oversee the care of someone who'd hurt him and his mother so deeply. Even if his father was a different man now, Cole still bore the scars of his childhood. Yet she'd seen the concern in his eyes when the nursing home had called regarding his father's injury.

There was no denying Cole Heinsohn was a complex man, burdened by his own past, all the while longing to create a better future for two little ones who'd somehow touched his life.

She was rolling the final pair of socks when she heard a piano playing. Yes, there was one in the living room, but this wasn't childlike banging, it was actual music. "Jingle Bells," To be exact.

Stepping back into the kitchen, she noted the empty table before continuing into the living room with its lace curtains and floral uphol-stered sofa. Max sat on the floor, playing with the dinosaurs Rae kept in the backpack. Lift-ing her gaze, she spotted Maggie sitting on the bench in front of the piano while a lovely ren-dition of the Christmas carol played from the upright.

Maggie knew how to play the piano? Even better than most adults?

Rae inched closer, pausing beside the key-board.

The girl promptly stopped and looked up, a worried expression on her sweet face. "I'm sorry."

"Oh, sweetie, you're not in trouble. That was beautiful." Rae joined her on the bench. "Where did you learn to play the piano?"

Maggie's dark eyes tentatively met Rae's. "She taught me."

At a loss, Rae said, "She?"

The girl hesitated for a long moment. "My other mama." Again, she looked up at Rae, though this time her eyes were brimming with tears. "Why did my daddy make her go away?"

Rae momentarily closed her eyes, grateful Maggie was finally opening up.

"Oh, baby." Rae took the precious child into her arms. "I wish I had an answer for you. There are some things in life that we'll never understand." Eyeing Max still playing obliviously on the floor, she cleared her throat and leaned back to gaze upon Maggie's sweet face. "I haven't told you this, but my mommy and daddy went away, too."

Maggie sobered. "They did?"

"Mmm-hmm."

"What did you do?"

"Well, I was older than you. But my little brother was still in school, so I had to take care of him."

Seemingly perplexed, Maggie cocked her head. "I thought Uncle Wes was your brother."

Rae couldn't help smiling. "He is. And he was once a boy."

The girl seemed to ponder the revelation. "Did you miss your mommy and daddy?"

Rae nodded. "I still do sometimes."

Maggie scowled. "I don't miss my daddy. He

was mean. Not like Mr. Cole. He's always nice. He plays with me and Max."

Even the kids could see how kind Cole was. So why did he think he could be like his father? "Yes, he is very nice."

"You should marry him," Maggie declared then nodded.

Oh, the simplicity of childhood. "He would make a good catch, wouldn't he?" Eager to be done with this part of the conversation, Rae said, "Maggie, how would you like to take piano lessons?" They could be just the therapy she needed. Plus, it would involve some time just for Maggie.

Those dark brown eyes grew wide, along with her smile. "I would love, love, love that."

"In that case, I'm going to do some checking around to see if we can't find someone to teach you."

Maggie threw her arms around Rae. "Thank you so much."

Rae hugged her back, blinking away tears. This was the breakthrough she'd been praying for. Rae had no idea how much the child was grieving her mother, but now that she knew, she was going to do everything in her power to help Maggie heal.

Her phone beeped in the other room. Sniffling, she released the girl. "You're welcome to keep playing, if you like."

Maggie nodded. "It's almost Christmas."

"It sure is." Rae smoothed a hand across the girl's back and checked on Max again, surprised he didn't want to play, too. Most kids couldn't resist pecking at a piano, whether they knew how to play or not.

Returning to the kitchen, she scooped up her phone to see a text from Cole.

What doll was it that Maggie wanted?

She tucked her curiosity aside and typed a reply.

A Country Girl doll by the name of Emma.

Moments later, a wavy bubble appeared on the screen, indicating he was typing.

Anticipation had Rae tapping her fingers against the side of the phone. Why would Cole be asking about the doll?

Finally, his response came through.

You can check it off your list.

It was followed by a picture of the very doll Rae hadn't been able to track down.

She could hardly believe it. Not only had he remembered, he'd actually gone out and found the doll she thought she'd never be able to find.

Yes sirree, Cole Heinsohn would make a great catch indeed. Sadly, after what she'd gone through with her ex, though, Rae had no interest in fishing.

Still, she wanted to do something for Cole to pay him back for all the kindness he'd showed her and the kids. And she couldn't think of a better way than to create some happy Christmas memories for him.

Yep, her efforts to give Maggie and Max the perfect Christmas had just been extended to Cole. The only problem might be getting him to participate. But with two cute little kids in her arsenal, he didn't stand a chance.

Armed with a plain cardboard box that concealed Maggie's doll, Cole paused beside his assistant's desk on Monday morning.

"Brenda, I have to drop something by the café." He gestured to the box. "Can I get you anything while I'm there? Some baked goods, perhaps?" Though it was an afterthought, he quickly tacked on that last part, lest he have to listen to another lecture about the woman's dislike of fancy coffee drinks.

The petite gray-haired woman he feared losing to retirement in the not too distant future looked up from her computer. "You sure know how to tempt a gal, don't you?"

He shrugged. "May as well get used to it. The holidays are almost here, so the temptations will abound."

"Don't I know it." She thought for a moment. "If there's anything pumpkin spice, I'm game. If not, I'll save the calories for all the pie I'm bound to stuff my happy self with on Thanksgiving."

He felt himself smile. "I'll see what I can do." Box in hand, he moved outside, noting the Christmas decorations going up across the street on the square. The large tree that would be lit at Saturday's Christmas kick-off parade appeared to be a work in progress while the large sleigh kids loved to play on still sat atop a flatbed trailer along the opposite side of the courthouse.

The crisp morning air helped clear the fog from his brain as he continued up the sidewalk. Since his time with Rae on Saturday, he'd felt drained. Embarrassed. Vulnerable.

Reaching for his collar, he loosened his tie. It wasn't like him to open up. He'd always kept a tight lid on his past, never divulging even the smallest amount of information about his family. The only person who knew the things

Rae now did was Tilly, and that was only because his mother had shared everything with her sister.

An old classmate waved from the cab of his pickup as he rolled past, and Cole returned the gesture. No doubt about it, he was completely out of his element when it came to Rae. She sparked emotions he'd never experienced before, igniting longings for things he knew he could never have. And he didn't like it one bit. So, after church yesterday, he'd checked in on his father then gotten into his truck and simply drove, trying to outrun the torturous thoughts and the urge to take Rae up on the lunch offer she'd extended in the church parking lot after the service.

Yet, no matter how far he drove, his mind kept going back to Rae and the kids. That was when he decided to go in search of the doll that had Rae so tied up in knots with worry. Not only was he eager to alleviate her burden, he wanted to see the smile on her pretty face when he presented it to her.

You're walking a mighty fine line.

Yes, he was. And if he wasn't careful, he might find himself doing something he'd end up regretting. If he were to hurt Rae…

He paused at the door to the café. *Lord, help me. I have no idea what I'm doing.*

The aromas of coffee and whatever today's lunch special were enveloped him as he entered the establishment he'd frequented more in the last few weeks than he had all year. And was that Christmas music he heard playing?

Voices drew his attention to a table near the counter where Rae and her friends Paisley, Christa and Wes's wife, Laurel, appeared deep in conversation.

Unexpected disappointment twisted his gut. This was a bad idea. He should have texted first to make sure she was available.

He started to turn for the door.

"Mr. Cole!" Max's voice was followed by the sound of small feet hurrying across the wood floor.

His heart swelled when he saw Maggie and Max closing in. "Well, good morning." Confused, he held up his free hand for a round of high-fives. "How come you two aren't at school?" He hoped they weren't sick. They didn't look sick.

Rae approached. "They have the whole week off for Thanksgiving."

"You don't say?" His gaze shifted to the kids. "Man, back when I was in school—" just saying those words made him feel ancient "—we only got *two* days off for Thanksgiving." He glanced from Maggie to her brother. "So, are you helping your mama?"

Max shook his head. "We're making Christmas ornaments." He reached for Cole's hand. "Come see."

He turned his attention to Rae. "I'm fine. You go back to what you were doing." With an emphatic Max dragging him deeper into the restaurant, Cole nodded to the women as he passed. "Morning, ladies."

"Morning," they responded in unison.

Laurel bounced her baby boy on her knee. "Good to see you again, Cole."

Nearing the next table, he spotted Mick's niece, Sadie, and a little blonde he assumed was Wes's daughter kneeling in their chairs as they hovered over an assortment of pipe cleaners and beads.

"Lookie, look!" Sadie held up a red-and-white beaded pipe cleaner bent to look like a candy cane.

"That's very nice," he said. "Did you make that?"

She nodded. "Don't tell Uncle Mickey, though. I want to surprise him."

"I see. In that case, I won't say a word."

"This is Sarah-Jane." Maggie acted like a regular little mother, patting the toddler on the back. "I'm helping her."

Cole felt a tug on the arm Max had finally released. Looking down, he found Max holding a red-and-green beaded candy cane, his dark eyes brimming with sincerity as he stared up at Cole.

"I made this one for you."

Emotion squeezed Cole's heart. The boy had gone from not trusting him to making him a gift.

He crouched to the boy's level. "Thank you very much, Max." Taking hold of it, he examined the heartfelt token.

"You can hang it on your Christmas tree," the boy said.

Cole didn't have the heart to tell the kid he'd never put up a Christmas tree. "I'm going to put this in a special place, where I can see it all the time." How he loved watching the boy's smile grow wide.

"All right, kiddos." Standing, Laurel inched closer with her baby boy on her hip. "Gather up your things."

Uncertainty creased Rae's brow as she watched her sister-in-law. "You're sure you want *all* of them?"

"Are you kidding?" Laurel slung a backpack over her shoulder. "You're doing me a favor. They'll keep Sarah-Jane entertained so I don't have to."

"If you say so." Rae looked worried. "But if they give you any trouble, just call and I'll be right there."

"They'll be fine," the blonde assured her.

Cole helped Max into his jacket. "You have fun, buddy."

One by one, they all moved out the door until he and Rae were alone.

He looked from the windows to Rae. "I didn't mean to chase your friends away."

"Don't be silly." She waved a hand, glancing at the box in his hand. "Paisley was just bringing us up to date on her wedding plans."

"And?"

"Everything's a go for December nineteenth. And I'm her maid of honor." Her gaze continued to bounce from the box to his face and back.

"At the castle?"

"Naturally." Her blue eyes sparkled as she pointed to the box. "Is that what I think it is?"

He placed the object of her interest on the nearest table. "Let's find out." With that, he lifted the flaps while she looked on.

Taking hold of the package inside, she pulled it out and examined it, her smile wide. "Maggie's going to be so happy." She gently touched the plastic covering. "Where did you find it?"

Hands in his pockets, he shrugged and

rocked back on the heels of his oxfords, enjoying her smile. "Austin."

"Austin!" She set the doll on the table. "What were you doing in Austin?" Seeming to catch herself, she added, "Not that it's any of my business." Her cheeks took on a deeper shade of pink.

"I went for a drive and the next thing I knew, I had pulled into one of those superstores and managed to snag the last two on the shelf."

Her brow furrowed. "Why two?"

"Let's just say I went a little overboard with my shopping."

She cocked her head. "How overboard?"

"My cart runneth over."

"Oh, my."

"Don't worry. I plan to put a good bit of it, including the second doll, into a toy bundle we can add to the silent auction. Though I did get some things for Maggie and Max, too."

She sent him an appreciative look. "You didn't have to do that."

"I wanted to." He hesitated a moment, gathering enough courage to finish what he wanted to say. "If it's all right with you, I'd like to help you with the kids' Christmas."

"If by helping you mean you'd like to participate in our Christmas activities as well as contribute to the kids' haul of presents, I think that's a wonderful idea." She glanced at the doll still in her hands, then, before he realized what was happening, she set the doll down and threw her arms around his neck. "Thank you so, so much." Her breath was warm on his ear, sending jolts of electricity racing through him.

"You're welcome."

Just as quickly as she'd hugged him, she pulled away. "Oh, guess what?"

Still reeling from her embrace, he simply stared at her.

"Maggie can play the piano." Excitement bubbled out of her in the form of a giggle. "When we were at the farmhouse yesterday, I heard Maggie playing the piano." She excitedly shared how Maggie had finally opened up.

"That's great news, Rae." One less burden for her to carry around.

"I promised her I'd find someone to give her lessons." Suddenly hesitant, she peered up at him. "Is it okay if she plays that piano at the house?"

"Of course. My mother would be thrilled to know someone was enjoying it. And if you haven't found an instructor already, I believe Rita Evans, the piano player at the church, still gives lessons."

"I didn't know that. I'll give her a call." Rae tucked the doll package back inside the box and heaved a sigh. "These past few days certainly have been a whirlwind of emotions."

Though he knew she was including him in her statement, he remained silent.

"Cole—" she faced him again "—we all have pasts. Thank you for sharing yours with me. I know it wasn't easy."

He eyed the door, trying to come up with an excuse to leave. He did not want to go down this road again.

"I just have one more question."

Clenching his teeth, he dared a look at her. "Which is?"

"Will you join the kids and me for Thanksgiving dinner at Paisley's?" Her smile was a playful one. Still, he couldn't help but wonder if she was simply taking pity on him.

He rubbed his chin. "I don't know. I—"

She held up a hand, cutting him off. "Crockett will be there with his kids, along with Wes, Laurel and their family, including Laurel's dad, Jimmy, not to mention Mick, Christa and Sadie. That means I'm the odd woman out." Lowering her hand, she continued. "So if you don't have any other plans, would you please be my plus-one?"

He simply stood there in amazement as the front door opened and the early lunch crowd trickled in. Rae was either desperate or really good at turning the tables on him. Whatever the case, he couldn't bring himself to say no.

"What time should I pick you up?"

Chapter Nine

Rae could hardly believe it. In addition to singing with the children's choir, Maggie was going to play piano in the church's Christmas concert.

After contacting Rita regarding lessons Monday afternoon, she'd asked Rae and the kids to stop by so she could evaluate Maggie's skill level. Rita had been so impressed, she'd invited Maggie to play "Jingle Bells" for the entire church.

Rae could hardly contain her enthusiasm. This was going to be an awesome Christmas, indeed, and not only for Maggie and Max. She planned to give Cole a bundle of Christmas memories he'd never forget, too, starting with trimming the tree.

"Who's ready to decorate the Christmas tree?"

A duo of delighted *me*s echoed from the back

seat of Cole's truck, adding to Rae's excitement. Finally, after months of planning, the Christmas season was officially here.

"Are you sure you wouldn't rather wait until tomorrow?" Cole glanced her way as he turned his truck into the deserted alley behind the café. "You know, *after* we've had a chance to digest that over-the-top Thanksgiving meal." He patted his trim midsection.

As usual, Paisley had outdone herself, offering up both turkey *and* ham, along with sweet potato casserole, dressing, roasted green beans, homemade cranberry sauce, scratch-made rolls and not one but three types of pie—pumpkin, pecan and apple. The looks on Maggie's and Max's faces when they'd seen all that food had been priceless.

"No way. This'll be just the exercise we need to work it all off." She glanced his way. "Could it be that you're regretting that second helping of pie?"

He parked alongside the stairs that led to her apartment. "Yep."

"Mama Rae put the tree up last night," said an excited Max as they hurried up the steps a few minutes later. "It's *huge*. And it already has lights."

Reaching the landing at the top, Cole looked

at her. "A prelit tree? I thought for sure you'd have a real one."

A gust of cool air tossed her hair as she shoved her key into the lock and twisted. "That would have been my preference, but for the sake of time, I opted to go with a very *real*-looking faux tree that can change from white to colored lights at the push of a button."

He held the door as the kids scurried inside, then waited for her to pass. "Let me guess, the kids wanted colored lights and you wanted white lights."

Shrugging out of her jacket, she said, "Compromise is always a good thing. Even if it costs a little more."

His reaction took her by surprise. Was that actually a chuckle she heard coming from Cole? She'd never heard him do that before.

"What about the cookies?" Maggie waited impatiently in the kitchen.

"Seriously?" Cole looked positively mortified. "After all that food?"

Rae brushed the girl's hair away from her sweet face. "That'll be our treat after we're finished. Along with some hot cocoa."

"I like hot cocoa." In the living room, Max parked himself beside the boxes of ornaments and Christmas decorations she'd dug out of the attic yesterday. Most hadn't been opened since she'd moved to Bliss almost four years ago, so it would be fun seeing her cherished mementos again.

Moving to the counter, she double-checked her list. She was determined to make sure everything was perfect. *Cookies, cocoa, music—*

She palmed her forehead. "No wonder it's so quiet in here. I almost forgot the music." She instructed her smart speaker to play some Christmas tunes. "Okay, there's just one more thing. You kids have a seat and I'll be right back." She hurried down the hall and retrieved a gift bag from her bedroom before rejoining them. Cole had settled on the leather sofa, one ankle perched atop the opposite knee.

While Andy Williams crooned about the most wonderful time of the year, the kids drew near as Rae joined them on the large area rug. No doubt they were curious as to what was in the festive bag. "You guys get the honor of putting the first ornaments on the tree."

Their faces lit up.

"I've picked out a special one for each of you."

Maggie's eyes sparkled. "You mean we get our own ornament?"

Rae nodded. "When I was a little girl, my mom and dad gave me and my brother an ornament every year. And you know what?"

"What?" the kids replied in unison.

"I still have mine, and you get to help me put them on *our* tree. So—" Rae reached into the bag and pulled out the first one "—Maggie, this is for you."

The girl looked at the picture on the box. "Aw, it's a penguin and a snowman. They're so cute."

Now on his knees, Max inched closer. "I wanna see mine."

Rae pulled out the next one. "Here you go, Max."

His smile grew bigger as he assessed the image on the box. "Mine has a penguin, too. And a polar bear." He hurried to his feet and took off toward the couch. "Look, Mr. Cole. I got my own ornament."

"That's pretty special, Max."

Again, Rae reached into the bag. "Well, what do you know? I have another ornament." She sent Cole a rather mischievous look. "I wonder who it's for?"

He looked skeptical. "Surely not for me."

"Then you would be incorrect, counselor, because it *is* for you." Stretching across the coffee table, she handed it to him, hoping he didn't think the teddy bear and little snowman too juvenile. But when she'd seen they were playing on a swing set with a curving slide, she couldn't resist.

He stared at it for a moment, a slow smile playing at his lips. "It's perfect."

Finally, she grabbed the ornament hooks from the bag and handed one to each of the kids before joining Cole on the sofa. "You're welcome to hang it on our tree, or you can take it home and put it on yours."

Something akin to embarrassment flashed across his face. "Considering I've never had a tree at my place, I think I'll add it to yours."

She supposed she couldn't fault the guy. A tiny tabletop tree had been the extent of her Christmas decorating in recent years. Then again, she went all-out at the café and had a large tree there.

Over the next hour, Bing Crosby, Perry Como, Amy Grant and countless other classic artists serenaded them as they unpacked her childhood memories and placed them on the tree. But when she unwrapped the layers of tissue paper from the final ornament, the words *Our First Christmas Together* sent her spirits plummeting. It was the one she'd bought the year she and Sean had married.

Why do I still have this?

"Is it time for cookies?" Maggie's words

jarred her from the onslaught of painful memories.

"Uh, sure. Let me go turn on the oven." Hurrying into the kitchen, she promptly tucked the ornament beneath a towel lying on the counter. She would not allow Sean to ruin this night. He'd robbed her of enough already.

Cole approached as she was punching the buttons on the oven. "Are you all right?"

Clearing her throat, she forced a smile. "Yeah, I just lost track of time, that's all. The kids picked out some of those ready-to-bake snowman cookies. They should be ready soon."

He watched her curiously. "You're sure you're okay?"

"Yes." Moving past him, she returned to the living room.

"Isn't it beautiful, Mama Rae?" Maggie wrapped her little arms around Rae's waist, chasing away the ache that threatened to spoil her evening.

"It sure is." She stroked the girl's silky hair. "You guys did a wonderful job."

"I can hardly wait to see Santa Saturday." Maggie peered up at Cole as he approached. "Are you going to the Christmas parade with us?"

He hesitated. "I hadn't really thought about it."

"Please, Mr. Cole." Max watched the man intently. "You gotta come."

"In that case, I guess I'm going."

"Yay!" the kids cheered in unison.

"Can we have cookies and cocoa now?" Max barely looked away from the tree.

"Sure."

"Can we watch a Christmas show?" Maggie watched her expectantly.

"A short one."

While Cole and the kids placed the cookie dough on a baking sheet, Rae filled a kettle with water. This was the scene she'd dreamed of her whole adult life. Yet she'd been so preoccupied helping Sean achieve his dreams that hers had all but died.

Before the Christmas cartoon was halfway through, the cookies had been devoured, everyone's cocoa cups were empty, and Maggie's and Max's eyelids had grown heavy.

Sitting on the couch with Cole, Rae said, "I need to get them to bed." She faced him now. "If you have to go, I understand."

"Why don't I stick around and give you a hand?"

Thankfully, the kids gave no argument, donning their pajamas and brushing their teeth in record time before crawling into bed.

Rae kissed each of them good-night before joining Cole in the kitchen.

"You look kind of tired yourself," he said. "Let me help you clean up so you can get to bed, too."

She continued into the living room to retrieve the Santa plate the cookies had been on, too drained to argue. "I appreciate that."

He gathered the cocoa mugs. "Looks like we're heading into the homestretch for the Mistletoe Ball."

"Don't remind me." She shuffled back into the kitchen.

"Why do you sound so defeated?" Setting the cups beside the sink, he turned on the water and began to rinse them. "It's not all on you, you know. We're in this together."

"Yeah, I know." She opened the dishwasher.

"Now don't go shrugging me off like that." He handed her the first mug. "The Mistletoe Ball is a team effort, not a solo act."

"But solo is all I've ever known."

He gave her a second mug before adding the other two himself. "Well, it's time you stop thinking like that." He reached for the towel on the counter, revealing the ornament she'd hidden earlier. "What's this?" The two cookies she'd eaten turned to lead in her stomach as he picked up the partially wrapped symbol of her failed marriage.

"It's nothing." Looking away, she rubbed her suddenly chilled arms. "I don't even know why I still have it."

He rested his hip against the counter. "As someone recently reminded me, we all have pasts. I would imagine the particular Christmas that ornament is associated with—" he gestured to the ornament "—would hold some good memories."

"I suppose." She added the plate to the dishwasher and closed the door, allowing her mind to drift back to that day and the extravagant Christmas at Sean's parents' house. "I was so excited to finally spend Christmas with a family again." She crossed her arms over her chest. "Sean and I had so many dreams. His dad owned a car dealership and Sean was poised to open his own. I ran the business office. Together, we had a singular focus. Working toward that dealership meant everything to us. And before we knew it, we'd achieved our dream. He was never satisfied, though. He always wanted more. Bigger. Better."

She drew in a shaky breath. "Let's sit in the living room." They moved to the sofa, where she grabbed the faux fur throw from the back and covered her legs. "We were closing in on our eleventh wedding anniversary when I began to suspect he was cheating. Money was going out faster than usual, yet I couldn't figure out why. Of course, when I confronted him, he denied everything." *Come on, Rae. We're partners in every way. Nobody gets me like you.* "Like a fool, I suggested we start a family. But he insisted the dealership was our baby. Soon, money was being unaccounted for again, so I hired a private investigator, who confirmed my suspicions."

Cole reached for her, his hand warm while hers felt like ice.

"I used to think I'd never experience anything worse than losing my parents. Sadly, I was wrong." She stared at their clasped hands, unwilling to risk falling apart if she looked him in the eye. "I know I'm better off without him. And my attorney saw to it that I came away a winner financially, but knowing that Sean's remarried and has three kids still hurts. He got the one thing I'd always wanted."

"A family."

She nodded.

The cushions gave way as Cole moved closer, his strong arms enveloping her.

The tears she'd been holding back now trailed down her cheeks as he pulled her close. For the first time in a long while, she allowed herself the luxury of being comforted—if only for a moment.

Pulling away, she wiped the moisture from her face. "I'm sorry."

"No, I'm sorry. I'm sorry your ex-husband didn't love you the way he vowed he would. I'm sorry he didn't embrace your dreams like you embraced his. But I'm so glad he's no longer a part of your life, because you deserve better."

"I think so, too." She let out a soft laugh and reached for a tissue from the box on the side table. "Thank you for letting me get that off of my chest. Now I won't be dwelling on it all night." Instead she'd likely be thinking about the sad silver-gray eyes of the man before her, wondering what it would take to make them come alive.

Cole parked in front of the nursing home Saturday afternoon, still reeling from his conversation with Rae on Thanksgiving night. He'd been an attorney for more than two decades. During that time, he'd encountered many emotional women. Usually, he just sat quietly until they were ready to continue. Not once had he felt the need to comfort any of them.

That hadn't been the case the other night. Seeing Rae's tears had nearly undone him. Not only had he wanted to make them disappear, but to make her so incredibly happy she'd never shed another tear.

As if that would ever happen.

He exited his truck and made his way into the lobby, nearly plowing into Susan Salinas, a former classmate and Bliss's current mayor.

"Sorry about that, Susan."

She waved him off. "No, I wasn't paying attention. How's your father doing? I heard he had another fall."

"He's improving. The skin tear on his arm is healing."

"I'm glad that's all it was. Their bones are so brittle at that age." Susan's mother was a resident of Loving Hearts, as well.

"Yes, they are." Eager to see his father before meeting Rae and the kids for the parade, he moved past Susan. "It's good to see you."

"Good to see you, too, Cole."

As he reached the hallway, he heard Susan call his name. He turned to find her approaching.

"I was wondering…" She paused, her gaze roaming from his head to his boots and back again. "By any chance, are you planning to attend the parade tonight?"

"As a matter of fact, I am."

"How tall are you?"

Why would she want to know that? "Six foot."

She nodded. "I thought you were about my husband's size."

He wasn't sure why that mattered.

"You see—" she hoisted the strap of her oversize leather purse onto her shoulder "—Kenny was supposed to be Santa for tonight's holiday kickoff, but he just called to tell me he's at the hospital getting his foot x-rayed." She huffed out a breath. "I told him not to get on that big ol' ladder without me there, but did he listen to me? Now he can't walk. That means I need to find another Santa and…well, you and Kenny are about the same size."

Cole simply stared at the woman. Surely, she wasn't implying that she wanted *him* to play Santa.

She sucked in a breath. "Cole, would you do me and the people of Bliss a huge favor and be our Santa for tonight's events?"

He could feel his eyes growing wider with each word. He was the worst possible candidate for the job.

"I know this is short notice, and I wouldn't ask you if it wasn't an emergency, but the kids so look forward to visiting with Santa and getting their little candy canes."

"I—" He rubbed the back of his neck. "I don't know, Susan."

"Oh, come on, Cole. You'd be great. You'll simply ride on the float and wave to the kids as you go by. Then, after overseeing the lighting of the Christmas tree on the square, you'll sit in the sleigh to visit with the kids."

Oh, he was aware how it played out. He also knew just how much Max and Maggie, in particular, were looking forward to seeing the man in red. Maggie had talked about nothing else since they'd decorated the tree. But Susan ought to be able to come up with someone else to take on the role.

Her husband is at the hospital. She doesn't have time to embark on an all-out search.

Susan's phone rang. Looking at the screen, she harrumphed before answering. "Kenny, I will be there just as quick as I can." She paused. "Yes, I am in the process of finding a new Santa." Another pause. "All right, hon. You try to relax, and I'll be there shortly." She ended the call, shaking her head. "If I didn't love that man so much, I'd wring his neck."

Cole had played high school football with Kenny and remembered when the couple had been voted homecoming king and queen.

Dark eyes peered up at him. "Cole, I'm a desperate woman. The parade starts in less than two hours."

And he was scheduled to meet Rae and the kids shortly before that. They'd have to go without him. Then again, did he really want to see the disappointment on Maggie's and Max's little faces if there was no Santa?

"The event won't be the same without Santa."

Cole's gut clenched. *Lord, this is so far out of my comfort zone.*

He sucked in a breath. "All right, I'll do it."

Susan looked up at him, blinking. "You will?"

"Fill me in on all the details before I change my mind."

An hour later, after he'd been briefed, provided with the proper attire and rehearsed his "ho, ho, ho," he called Rae to let her know what was going on.

"Oh, this is priceless." She laughed. "I am going to take *so* many pictures. Then, after Santa heads back to the North Pole, you can stop by here for some cookies and hot cocoa."

"Given that I don't have time for dinner, I'll need something more substantial than that."

By the time the parade started at six, he was looking forward to the chicken enchiladas Rae promised to have waiting for him. He waved as the flatbed trailer adorned with a cardboard fireplace, a Christmas tree with presents and tons of lights rolled down Bliss's Main Street with the aid of a pickup truck, thankful for the white hair and beard that, hopefully, made him unrecognizable.

Christmas songs, courtesy of the high school marching band, filled the pleasantly cool evening air, and as they neared the square, the aromas from various food vendors awakened his appetite. Everything from street tacos and barbecue to hot chocolate and spiced cider carried on a gentle breeze.

People wearing broad smiles and festive sweaters lined both sides of the street. Children bounced with anticipation, their eyes alight with excitement. Finally, he spotted Maggie and Max standing with Rae in front of the café, and the joy on their little faces made him glad he'd given in to Susan's request. He looked right at the kids and waved, while Rae snapped picture after picture.

Finally, after circling the square, the float came to a stop and he moved on to the Christmas tree lighting with the aid of a couple of elves he recognized as chamber of commerce employees. Once the tree was lit, he was escorted to Santa's sleigh where a line of kids already stretched along the walkway. This was going to take a while.

Shoving aside his trepidation, he shot up a prayer, asking God to make him a blessing and not a disappointment to the kids.

One by one, children of all ages made their way into the sleigh, accepting their candy canes and expressing their wishes. Most sat beside him, though he was handed a couple of babies purely for the photo op. Talk about out of his element. Thankfully, only one was screaming and neither of them had wiggled out of his grip, despite their best efforts. To his surprise, he found himself kind of enjoying the gig.

The line had shrunk to only a handful of kids when Maggie and Max finally approached the sleigh.

"Ho, ho, ho." Cole lowered his voice, hoping they wouldn't recognize him. "Well, hello there."

Maggie stepped forward right away. "Hi, Santa."

"Come on in here, young lady." Cole patted the seat beside him, and Maggie wasted no time. Handing her a candy cane, he said, "Tell ol' Santa what you'd like for Christmas."

"I want an Emma Country Girl doll."

"I hear she's very popular."

Maggie nodded. "*And*—" she leaned closer,

cupping her hand around her mouth "—I want Mama Rae to marry Mr. Cole."

He froze, his gut tightening. Did she think he and Rae were a couple? Sure, they were spending a lot of time together, but... *God, how do I respond to this?*

He cleared his throat, willing his shock aside. "I'm sorry, young lady, but Santa doesn't have control over matters of the heart."

Maggie blinked up at him. "Why not? Mama Rae says Mr. Cole would make a good catch."

His insides warmed as his gaze inadvertently drifted to the woman taking countless photographs, a smile tugging at the corners of his mouth. "Did she now?"

Coming to his senses, he looked to Max, ready to change the subject. "Is that your brother?"

"Mmm-hmm." The girl motioned Max forward. "Come talk to Santa."

Eyes round, the kid shook his head.

"It's okay, Max," his sister encouraged. "It's just Santa."

While most kids viewed Santa as a good guy, in Max's mind, he was still a man. And men had to earn Max's trust. It was something that took more than a few seconds.

Cole scooted as far over on the seat as he could without falling out of the sleigh before addressing Maggie. "Perhaps he'd feel more comfortable if you stayed here with him."

"Come on, Maxy," Maggie encouraged once again. "I'll stay with you."

Rae knelt beside the boy, likely whispering reassuring words the way Cole's mother had always done with him.

Finally, the boy inched toward the sleigh.

"Merry Christmas, Max." Cole tried to keep his voice upbeat while still disguising it. And while he normally would have offered a hand to help the kid up, he held off, preferring Max come on his own terms.

When the boy finally sat, Cole passed him a candy cane. "What's on your Christmas list, young man?"

Max looked from him to Maggie and Rae then back to Maggie. "You can go." The words were spoken so quietly, as though they were meant for Maggie's ears only.

"Okay." His sister promptly stepped out of the sleigh, leaving a gaping space between Cole and Max.

Not wanting him to feel rushed, Cole said, "Take your time, young man. Whenever you're ready is fine with me."

He held his breath as Max inched closer.

Stopping a short distance away, but close enough to be heard, he met Cole's gaze. "I want to stay with Mama Rae forever." The yearning in his dark eyes had Cole's throat clogging with emotion.

Before he could respond, the boy bounded off the sleigh and returned to Rae's side, leaving Cole with a deep desire to make Maggie's and Max's dreams come true, yet keenly aware that both were out of his hands. True, he might be able to help Rae as she sought permanent custody of the kids, but it wasn't a guarantee, and Maggie's request was impossible. Cole wasn't marriage material. He couldn't risk destroying the lives of people he cared about.

No, he'd help Rae give those two the best Christmas ever, one that would leave them with unforgettable memories. Then he would fade into the distance and pray they'd become the permanent family they deserved to be. He'd miss them terribly, but if he didn't step away, he'd find himself longing for things that could never be.

Chapter Ten

Everything that could have gone wrong with Rae's week had done just that.

First thing Monday morning, Adrian Hawkins, the now lone member of the live auction committee, called saying she had the flu, leaving Rae in charge of making sure all of the live auction donations were received, on top of the silent auction items she was already overseeing.

On Wednesday, her food delivery was delayed due to a broken-down truck. Instead of the usual morning delivery, it arrived after the kids got home from school, leaving her little time to get things squared away before she had to pack up the kids and rush to the church for Maggie and Max's concert rehearsal. Thankfully, Cole had offered to take the few auction items people had dropped by the café to the castle for her, removing that from her plate.

As if all that weren't enough, an unusually high number of people were requesting pickups of their auction donations. Throw in Maggie's piano lessons, trips to the farmhouse so the kids could expend energy, laundry and countless other tasks that cropped up, and Rae was going nowhere fast. So with roughly twenty-eight hours remaining until the Mistletoe Ball, outstanding auction items that still needed to be collected and a ballroom that had yet to be decorated, the last thing she needed was a broken refrigerator in the café.

Even the Christmas tree by the front window and the lively rendition of *"Sleigh Ride"* coming from a nearby speaker failed to settle her nerves as her gaze moved from the repairman's truck to her watch on Friday afternoon. If this fellow didn't hurry, she was going to be late getting Maggie and Max from school.

"All right, miss." The repairman emerged from the kitchen as she filled the last of the salt and pepper shakers. "Looks like your unit needs a new compressor, which I'll have to order."

Standing at the counter, she felt the tentacles of angst tighten. "How long is that going to take?"

"I should have it by Tuesday."

"Tuesday? What about all the food?" Her apartment refrigerator wouldn't hold half of it.

The balding man who looked to be in his late fifties held up a hand. "Now, now. I've gotcha covered. Let me grab something from my truck and I'll do a quick patch job that'll hold you till then."

She slowly exhaled the breath she'd been holding. *Thank you, Jesus.*

He slipped through the front door as her phone rang. Looking at the screen, she noted the local number. Folks had been calling all day regarding tomorrow morning's auction drop-off at the castle. "Hello?"

"Hi, this is Mary Stoval. My husband, Bradley, promised y'all a fire pit for the Mistletoe Ball auction."

Rae remembered. They were counting on the custom piece to bring some substantial bids. "Yes." She rubbed her forehead. If they were backing out now—

"Bradley got tied up on a welding job up in Fort Worth and won't be home until early next week."

Rae's blood pressure crept up another notch. When she'd called earlier in the week, he said he'd bring it by the castle tomorrow during the established 8:00-10:00 a.m. drop-off window.

"The good news is the fire pit is ready,"

Mary continued. "The bad news is I have no way to get it to you. It won't fit in my SUV."

That meant it likely wouldn't fit into Rae's, either. "Mary, let me do some checking and I'll call you back."

The door opened as she ended the call, but instead of the repairman, Cole strolled in.

Wearing her favorite navy pinstripe suit, he paused on the opposite side of the counter. "How're things—?" His gaze narrowed. "Something's wrong."

More like a gazillion things.

He eyed the returning repairman. "And I have a feeling whatever he's up to is just the tip of the iceberg." How could he possibly know her so well when Tilly had only been gone for a month?

"My refrigerator is on the fritz. He's working on a temporary fix until the part comes in next week."

As the repairman disappeared into the kitchen, Cole shoved a hand through his hair and rounded the counter to join her. "You know, you keep telling me you have everything under control. I should have known you were holding out on me." He reached for her hands. "Just tell me what to do. Whatever it takes to alleviate your burden, I can do."

Whether it was the warmth of his touch, or

the way his gorgeous eyes bored into her, she actually believed him. The Cole she'd come to know wasn't afraid to help others. She was the one with the problem. While she wasn't a control freak, letting go was tough because she'd never had anyone to pick up the slack when she fell short. Not since her parents died, anyway. She was the one who'd pushed Wes to do his schoolwork. It had been she who'd made sure Sean's financials were in order so his dream of owning a dealership could become a reality.

Stepping away, Rae let out a sigh and began recapping the shakers. "The to-do list just keeps getting longer."

He picked up a shaker and screwed the lid on. "Tell me everything on your list."

"Well, once he's finished in the kitchen, I have to pick up the kids then run by Wanda Parker's to get the quilt she made and Cathy Hoefler's for a basket of homemade jams and pickled stuff."

His smile was a slow one. "Pickled stuff, huh?"

"Stop." She elbowed him. "And I just got a call from the wife of the guy who promised that nice fire pit."

"Brad Stoval."

"He's stuck in Fort Worth and Mary has no way to get it to us."

"That's fine. I know where they live. I'll run out there and pick it up."

She grimaced. "I hate to make you do that."

"You're not *making* me do anything. Tilly asked me to assist you, so quit thwarting me." Watching her again, he asked, "What else?"

"Decorate the ballroom and set up the auction displays." A groan escaped her lips. "There's no telling how long that's going to take, but I'm pretty sure we're looking at a long night."

"I'll be at the castle first thing tomorrow to oversee the deliveries." He added another lid. "Please tell me you're not planning to put in a full day at the café."

With the last shaker complete, she grabbed the tray. "One of the girls offered to hold down the fort, but I don't know."

He watched her as she moved to the opposite counter. "Do yourself a favor and let your staff take care of things for the day. If there's a problem, they can call. The castle isn't that far away." When she didn't respond, he said, "I'm serious, Rae. Not only do I want you to enjoy yourself at the ball, stress will just wear you down. If you're worn out, you're more susceptible to illness. And I'm fairly certain you do not want to be sick during the holidays."

Why did he have to make so much sense? "All right, you've made your case."

"Good. So here's the plan—"

"Excuse me? I'm the one who's supposed to be in charge."

"I'm declaring you temporarily incompetent."

She squared her shoulders. "What? You can't—"

"I can and I will." His stern expression left no room for argument. "While you finish up here, I'll head to the Stovals'. You grab the kids, the quilt and Cathy's basket and then we'll meet at the castle and formulate our next plan of attack." He made it sound so simple.

"You think you've got this all figured out, don't you?"

"Only the next few hours. Now, call Mary and Paisley and tell them when to expect us. The kids are going to need snacks and toys. Have you got their backpack ready?" What had gotten into him?

"Right over there." She pointed to a chair near the counter.

"Do you want me to stay in case you have to get the kids before he's done?"

"No, I'm good."

One dark brow lifted in doubt.

With a heavy sigh, she whisked past Cole to the kitchen door. "Sir, how much longer do you think you'll be?"

"About four-and-a-half minutes."

She couldn't help chuckling. Making her way to Cole, she said, "See?"

"In that case—" he moved in the direction of the door "—I will let you know when I'm on my way back."

As she waited in the pickup line twenty minutes later, her mind kept revisiting the feel of Cole's hands enveloping hers. So strong and protective.

I'm declaring you temporarily incompetent.

She couldn't help laughing. Who did he think he was?

Someone looking out for your best interests.

That, she couldn't deny. Talk about unfamiliar territory. When was the last time anyone had been there for her?

Maggie and Max appeared, interrupting her thoughts. She informed them of her plans and gave them their snacks. They were thrilled to learn they'd be going to the castle. First things first, though.

She stopped by Cathy's before continuing to Wanda's, where the woman nearly talked Rae's ear off. Once again, Cole came to her rescue, calling to let her know he'd just passed the city limit sign, giving her the opportunity for a quick escape.

By the time she made it to Renwick Castle,

Cole was backing his truck into the drive. She parked inside the gate before helping the kids out.

They ran to greet Cole as he emerged from the cab. "Mr. Cole!" they cheered in unison.

After a round of high-fives, his gaze drifted to Rae. "Mission accomplished?"

"Yes. I just need to unload and then we can focus on the ballroom."

The front door opened and Paisley emerged from the three-story stone structure with towers at each corner and those square battlement cutout things along the roof. "That was faster than I anticipated." She glanced from Cole to Rae. "Darlin', how *did* you manage to get away from Wanda so quickly?"

Rae pointed to Cole. "One perfectly timed phone call was all it took."

Paisley sent him an approving smile. "Well done, counselor."

While Cole opened his tailgate, Paisley linked her arm through Rae's. "Before you unload, I have something I'd like to show you."

Rae eyed her friend, unsure whether she should be concerned or not. "What is it?"

"Follow me."

She turned to call the kids, but Cole cut her off.

"I'll keep an eye on them."

With that, she and Paisley made their way into the entry hall with its limestone floors and wood-paneled walls, past the Texas cattle barons' portion of the museum, then up the grand staircase to the second floor where the ballroom was located.

"It appears Cole is taking his co-chair duties very seriously," said Paisley.

"Yeah, he's been quite helpful." *He could've done more if you'd have let him.*

He's a busy man who has his father to worry about.

"The kids seem to like him."

"I know." Rae followed her friend down the corridor to the double doors that led to the ballroom. "He even managed to win Max over." So what would she do once Christmas was over and Cole had no reason to come around anymore?

"Where will they be tomorrow night?"

"Wes and Laurel offered to keep them."

Reaching for the door handle, Paisley sent her a mischievous smile. "Are you ready?"

"Ready for what? You never said what you wanted to show me."

"Oh. Well, in that case." Paisley flung open one heavy wooden door.

Rae moved inside, her jaw dropping. Not only had Paisley set up the Christmas tree as promised, greenery adorned with hundreds of tiny white lights graced every window and the massive fireplace. But she hadn't stopped there. The tables were all in place, dressed with white linens, and the rustic centerpieces Rae had dropped off last week were simply gorgeous. The only things missing were the auction items.

Still trying to take it all in, she faced her friend. "Paisley, I can't believe you did this."

"We can change or move anything you want." She came alongside Rae.

"Are you kidding? This is perfect." She looked up to meet Paisley's sparkling eyes. "Do you realize how much time you saved me?"

"That's precisely what we were hoping for."

Still in shock, Rae cast her friend a quizzical look. "'We'?"

"This was Cole's idea." Paisley smiled. "When he stopped by on Wednesday, I mentioned how eager I was to see the space decorated and that I was tempted to do it myself. He said you'd had a busy week and gave me the go-ahead. Said we could always change things if you didn't like it, but if you did, it was one less thing for you to do."

A strange giddiness bubbled in Rae's belly. "He…he said that?"

Her friend nodded. "Feels kind of nice to

have someone care about your well-being, doesn't it?"

Thoughts of Cole's determination to not only help Max but to join with her to give the kids a Christmas to remember played across her mind. Not to mention the play area he had built, how he'd found Maggie's doll, and now had stepped in this week to lessen her burden. It all felt so... wonderful. And that was the scariest thing of all.

After tonight, Rae could finally relax. That's what Cole hoped, anyway. He was looking forward to spending the rest of the holiday season with her and the kids. Until recently, he'd never realized how enjoyable Christmas could be. But things were different through the eyes of a child. There was so much wonder and anticipation.

Then there was their foster mom, who tried to carry way too much on her petite shoulders. He'd done whatever he could think of this past week to help alleviate Rae's stress. Granted, getting her to share those things that weighed on her wasn't easy, so he'd kept his eyes peeled, looking for opportunities to ease her burden. So the smile she'd worn as she'd wandered the fully decorated ballroom last night had him longing to do more. Because he was quickly discovering he liked making her smile.

This morning's deliveries had gone off without a hitch and, by the time they'd departed the castle at two this afternoon to get cleaned up for tonight, everything, including the auction items, was ready to go. The only glitch was the auctioneer's delayed arrival, which wasn't so bad since it allowed more time for bids on the silent auction items.

"All right, folks, you've dug deep tonight, but let's dig a little deeper." The forty-something auctioneer stood at the podium on the stage set up at one end of the room. "We want to bless some youngsters this Christmas and, ladies and gentlemen, we've saved the best for last. Our final item up for bid is an evening at Minute Maid Park when the Houston Astros take on the Texas Rangers this coming May. The package includes a private suite with tickets for up to ten people."

The guests oohed and aahed.

"Along with parking *and* catering." The man pulled a handkerchief from his breast pocket and tipped his gray felt Stetson back just enough to wipe his brow. "Folks, this is one doozy of a deal."

Standing off to one side, Cole scanned the

brightly lit ballroom full of guests, noting many of the men straightening in their seats, eager to scoop up the coveted prize for a bargain-basement price.

"We'll start the bidding at five hundred dollars." There was barely a pause before the auctioneer continued. "We have five hundred. Do I hear six?"

Soon, the man was talking so fast, Cole was hard-pressed to understand a word. By the time he finally caught on, the number had grown to two thousand dollars and two men were going back and forth.

Rae came alongside Cole, making his heart race. Her dark curls spilled over the shoulders of her red satin-and-lace dress, giving her a very regal look—not at all like the Rae he was used to seeing. While she'd always been pretty, this Rae commanded attention. And whether he liked it or not, she'd definitely captured his.

Nudging his elbow, she said, "I've never seen bids this high."

He leaned toward her until his mouth was beside her ear. Her sweet fragrance made him want to linger. "And you were worried."

She looked up at him with a bashful smile that threatened to steal his breath.

Clearing his throat, he said, "Did you post the winners for the silent auction?"

Her blue eyes sparkled. "Yes. It was a record-breaker."

"Twenty-five hundred dollars." The auctioneer's clear announcement had them turning his way. "Do I hear twenty-six hundred?" His gaze scanned the ballroom. He reached for his gavel. "Going once." Another quick perusal. "Going twice." A final once-over and the gavel fell. "Sold to the gentleman in the red bow tie."

Rae squeezed Cole's arm. "I won't know for sure until we tally everything, but I think we might have shattered an all-time record tonight." She motioned for him to follow her onto the stage. After thanking the auctioneer, she moved to the microphone. "Ladies and gentlemen, if you'll pardon the pun, y'all knocked it out of the ballpark tonight."

Laughter rippled across the room.

"Thanks to your generosity, foster children throughout the county are going to have an extra-special Christmas this year, so give yourselves a big round of applause."

The room erupted. When it finally quieted, she continued. "Cole and I will be at the table in the hall to collect your payments. And now—" she motioned toward his client in the corner beside the stage "—we're going to turn things over to our wonderful DJ, so the dance floor is yours. Enjoy!"

The lights dimmed and Cole offered his hand as they moved down the steps, Rae's touch setting off a strange sensation that seemed to radiate from his core. When they reached the cashier table, there was already a line of people eager to pay.

Over the next hour, an eclectic mix of dance tunes spilled from the ballroom behind them, everything from country to pop and even some Christmas tunes. And the longer he worked beside the beautiful woman in red, the more he longed to get her on the dance floor. Not that he'd had much practice dancing, save for a few times with his mother and aunt Tilly, but it was an opportunity he couldn't resist.

Paisley and Crockett approached the table.

"You two have set the bar pretty high for our inaugural event," said Crockett.

"Thanks in part to your lovely fiancée." Rae gestured to her friend.

Paisley promptly held up her hands. "No, no. I just did a little decorating. You did everything else."

"Actually, we have Tilly to thank for most of it," said Rae.

"Don't be so modest," said Cole. "You put

in a lot of hard work." Not to mention weeks of worry.

She cocked her head in his direction. "I could say the same thing about you."

Notes of "Rockin' Around the Christmas Tree" drifted from the ballroom.

"You're right. We should celebrate." He turned his attention to Crockett and Paisley. "Would you two mind holding down the fort here for a few minutes while I take this vision in red for a celebratory spin on the dance floor?"

"Not at all." Paisley moved beside her friend.

Panic flitted across Rae's face. "Are you sure? I mean, there are still some outstanding payments."

"Darlin', I've run many a business. I'm certain I can figure this out. If there are any problems, we'll find you."

Rae stood, albeit rather reluctantly. So, before she could change her mind, Cole took her by the hand and whisked her into the now dimly lit ballroom.

The dance floor was full, but he managed to find them a spot near the center. He'd barely initiated a couple of push moves when the song transitioned to Bing Crosby's "White Christmas." The DJ must have read his mind.

He slipped an arm around Rae's waist and eased her closer. "Congratulations. Not only did you survive, the ball was a rousing success."

Pink tinged her cheeks. "Only because you helped me."

"The pleasure was all mine." Looking into her eyes, he took a deep breath. "So what do we do now that the ball is over? Almost over, anyway."

"Well, there are three weeks till Christmas, so I still have plenty on my list. Starting with the concert at church tomorrow night."

"I plan to be there."

"You do?" Her eyes searched his, making him wonder if, maybe, she didn't want him to attend.

"Yes. I want to hear the kids sing and see Maggie play her song."

Her smile was a nervous one. "They're both pretty excited. They'll be happy you're there."

But what about Rae? Nothing she'd said indicated *she* wanted him there. On the contrary, he felt as though she was pulling away emotionally. Something he should be grateful for, right? Instead, it made him sad.

"Cole?" She looked him square in the eye. "I know you said you wanted to help with the kids' Christmas, but you've helped me so much this week."

She was retreating. Now that the ball was over, there was no need for them to be together. And given all he'd shared with her, he couldn't blame her. Still, he was really looking forward to the concert, the gingerbread houses and all those things he was getting to enjoy with Maggie and Max.

His stomach knotted, his hold on her loosening. "I helped because I wanted to, not because I had to. Just like I *want* to see the kids perform at the church. And as far as me helping with the kids' Christmas, I'm actually enjoying the holiday season, something I don't think I've ever been able to do before."

"Really?"

"Rae, if you don't want me to come around anymore, I understand. But don't go making up things out of thin air to make yourself feel better about it." He felt her body stiffen.

"That's not what I was doing."

"Then what were you doing?"

"Trying to give you an out."

"I don't need an out. If I *can't* or *don't* want to do something, you can count on me to be straight with you. And I'd appreciate it if you'd extend me the same courtesy."

The corners of her mouth tilted upward. "So, the truth, the whole truth, and nothing but the truth, huh?"

"Something like that, yes."

"I'm sorry, Cole. I wasn't trying to hurt you. I was just—"

"Protecting yourself?"

Her expression turned serious again. "You know me too well."

"No, definitely not well enough. Though I'd like to."

"So, later this week—" she peered up at him, looking rather shy "—the kids and I are planning to take some Christmas cookies to a shut-in."

"Always a nice gesture. Do you have anyone in mind?"

"Yes, but I need your opinion."

He looked at her curiously.

"Would it be okay if we took them to your father? We'd want you to go with us, of course."

He was taken aback. She didn't know his father. On the contrary, all she knew about Leland was what Cole had shared with her, most of which wasn't very flattering. Yet she was willing to reach out to the man in an act of kindness.

"I believe he would like that very much."

"Good. And then next Sunday we're going

to decorate gingerbread houses." Her fingers grazed the lapel on his jacket. "Care to join us?"

"You had me at gingerbread." He should be shaking in his boots. Instead, he could hardly wait.

Chapter Eleven

People were watching Rae and Cole as they slipped into a pew near the piano, toward the front of the sanctuary, Sunday evening. No doubt some of the busybodies would assume she and Cole were a couple. Not that Rae cared. Let them think what they wanted. She and Cole were just friends.

Not that you wouldn't mind something more.

That was not true. She frowned and plopped down on the cushioned pew. Okay, maybe a little bit of it was true, but still, she was perfectly happy with her life the way it was. Being a mother was the most fulfilling role she'd ever taken on. Certainly more gratifying than her marriage had ever been.

That didn't mean she didn't enjoy Cole's company, though. His desire to make Maggie's and Max's lives a little better was very endearing. She almost chuckled, thinking back on the way he'd talked about them last night on the dance floor. Had she ever seen him so emphatic? She wouldn't be making any more assumptions where the handsome attorney was concerned. Or at least not voicing them.

She leaned toward him. "Everything looks so festive." Faux candles flickered atop candelabra that rose out of groupings of bright red poinsettias along each side of the stage, near the piano and organ, and continued down the trio of steps. The baptistery was flanked by giant evergreen wreaths with twinkling white lights and shimmering red ribbon, the perfect accompaniment to the silhouetted nativity illuminating the back wall of the baptistery.

"'Tis the season," he responded.

Yes, it was. Her favorite season, and she could hardly wait to see her babies perform. They'd both been practicing so hard.

When Cole's gaze lifted, she turned to see Wes, Laurel and baby Wyatt approach.

"Merry Christmas!" Rae stood to greet her sister-in-law with a hug before snagging her five-month-old nephew from his daddy's arms. "Let me see this outfit." She held him at arm's length to view the red-and-black buffalo-checked sleeper sporting the cutest little moose wearing a Santa hat. "You are the cutest thing." She hugged him close and peppered him with kisses until he giggled. "That is my favorite sound in the whole world."

She was still getting her share of baby snuggles when Paisley, Crockett, Christa and Mick joined them. Rae couldn't help thinking how her and her friends' lives had changed in the last couple of years. Sarah-Jane, Laurel's almost-three-year-old, who'd turned out to be Rae's blood niece when it was revealed that Wes was the child's father, had been the only child in their group for the longest time. Now Christa was Mom to Mick's niece Sadie. Crockett's kids, Mackenzie and David, had readily welcomed Paisley into their family, and Rae had Maggie and Max. And every one of them, save for little Wyatt, was performing tonight.

Rae's heart was full as they all settled into the same pew. God had blessed her and her friends beyond measure.

Her gaze drifted to Cole, who sat to her left at the end of the pew. She was glad God had brought him into her and the kids' lives. He genuinely cared about Maggie and Max and went out of his way to show it. He was nothing at all like the man who had raised him. It broke her heart that he'd allowed his past to rob him of the joy of becoming a father. While he might doubt himself, she knew with every fiber of her being that he would make a wonderful dad.

The doors to the left and right of the stage opened, allowing children from toddlers to teens to file into the sanctuary. Their smiling faces spoke of the joy of the season.

Max spotted her, waving to get her attention, just like every other child who sought out their parents, except for the older ones who were too cool to risk embarrassment.

The directors herded the children into the front pews. Once everyone was settled, the piano came to life with a rousing rendition of "Joy to the World." Soon everyone was singing along.

Beside her, a rich baritone rang out loud and clear. She had no idea Cole had such a lovely voice. It was the kind that made her want to listen rather than sing.

After a brief welcome from Pastor Kleinschmidt, the lights dimmed and the adult choir on the stage sang a medley of popular Christmas tunes. Then it was the children's turn. Max and Maggie looked so cute in the special outfits she'd gotten them just for the occasion and beamed as they took their places. Sarah-Jane wasn't quite sure what to make of things, so Maggie took hold of her little hand, as if to say, "We're in this together."

If the adoption went through as Rae hoped, Sarah-Jane and Wyatt would be Maggie and Max's cousins. *Lord, please allow my dream to become a reality.*

As the kids sang "Away in a Manger," Rae vacillated between tears and laughter. Seeing her kids sing their little hearts out warmed her, but when one little boy decided to leap off the stage and hightail it to his parents, the whole room chuckled. Despite the interruption, they made it through "Happy Birthday, Jesus" without incident.

After the hand bell choir, it was Maggie's turn at the piano. She proudly stood from her seat and marched onto the stage in her red-velvet dress with the red-and-green-plaid sash.

Leaning toward Cole, Rae whispered, "I'm nervous for her."

"Don't be." His breath was soft on her ear. "You've heard her practice. She's got this."

Rae held her breath as Maggie sat on the bench, the camera on her phone at the ready.

Finally, Rita nodded to Maggie, signaling her to start.

Maggie's hands went to the keyboard, though she simply stared at them.

"We're ready, Maggie," Rita said from beside the stage. "Go ahead and play."

Again, the girl sat frozen.

Rae's insides tightened as she leaned into Cole. "She looks terrified."

He didn't say a word but watched intently as Rita moved onto the stage to speak with Maggie.

The girl nodded and Rita returned to the front of the stage, but Maggie remained still.

Before Rae knew what was happening, Cole stood and moved to the stage. He continued up the steps, past the poinsettias and around the piano.

Maggie looked up at him, though Rae couldn't see her face.

Cole smiled and sat beside her. He said something, though it was impossible to hear. Maggie responded, but again, Rae had no clue what they were saying.

Again, Cole spoke.

Maggie's smile grew wide. She nodded, looked at her hands and began to play. "Jingle Bells" had never sounded more beautiful.

When she finished, applause filled the sanctuary as Cole escorted her back to her seat.

The choir had begun singing by the time he settled beside Rae again. She leaned toward him, curiosity getting the best of her. "What did you say to her?"

"I simply asked her to play for me. So she did." He leaned back then, taking in the choir as if his actions were no big deal. But to her and Maggie, they were huge.

With a simple question, he'd not only helped Maggie overcome her fear, but made Rae want to cast hers aside, as well. Cole Heinsohn was unlike any man she'd ever known, and if she didn't guard her heart, she was going to find herself in major trouble.

This was a bad idea.

Cole aimed his truck in the direction of the nursing home early Friday evening, suddenly regretting his decision to allow Rae and the kids to visit his father. What if the good-humored Leland disappeared and the father Cole remembered decided to return? With dementia, anything was possible. If Leland so much as raised his voice to Rae or the kids, Cole would never forgive himself for putting them in such a position.

"I have good news."

He glanced at Rae in the passenger seat, grateful for a reprieve from his torment.

"They finally replaced the compressor on my refrigerator today," she continued, "*and* I mailed all of the thank-you cards." Her smile was wide. "I appreciate your willingness to help me with them."

They'd spent the last two evenings working

to get them knocked out. "And I appreciate you for providing a script I could copy."

He'd penned the words so many times, he'd heard them in his sleep last night. *Thank you for your donation to Bliss's Mistletoe Ball. Because of you, foster children throughout the county will have a Christmas to remember.* "I guess that wraps up everything pertaining to the ball?"

"Except for a final report to Tilly, but that can wait until she gets back. Any idea when that might be?"

"Next week will be six weeks, but the last I heard, she was debating whether or not to stay through Christmas."

Rae adjusted the plastic-wrap-covered platter of decorated cookies in her lap. "She may as well. It would only be another week or so."

"How much farther?"

Cole eyed Max in the rearview mirror. "We're almost there, buddy."

"Who are we giving the cookies to?"

Rae twisted to face the boy. "His name is Mr. Leland. He's a friend of Mr. Cole's."

He and Rae had decided not to tell the kids Leland was his father. If they were to mention anything about Cole being his son, the man would only be confused.

Cole's chest tightened when he pulled into

the parking lot of Loving Hearts. *God, please let this be a good experience for all of us.*

When they made it into the lobby, Rae paused beside the Christmas tree and knelt in front of the kids. "I want you two to be on your best behavior. Remember, we're here to spread Christmas cheer and brighten someone else's day, okay?"

"Cookies always make me happy," said Max.

Rae mussed his hair as she stood. "That's because you're my little cookie monster." She turned her attention to Maggie. "Would you like to carry the cookies, sweetie?" She held out the tray.

"Uh-huh." She took hold. "I promise to be very careful."

"I know you will." Rae gave the girl a brief hug before they started down the hall.

"If they had a piano, I could play for Mr. Leland," the girl said.

"I'm sure he would enjoy that." Cole walked alongside her, thinking of how his mother's piano playing often calmed his father.

When they reached Leland's room, Cole knocked on the door before poking his head inside. "Leland? Are you up for some company?" He held his breath.

"Well, hello there, young fella. Come on in."

"I brought some friends with me. Do you mind?"

"Not at all. The more, the merrier."

Cole motioned Rae and the kids into the room. "This is my friend Rae."

She knelt beside the man's wheelchair. "It's very nice to meet you, Leland."

"Pleasure's all mine." His gaze drifted to the kids. "And who are these two youngsters?"

"This is Maggie and her brother, Max," said Cole.

"We brought you some cookies." Still holding the platter, Maggie moved toward the man. Her sneaker bumped the toe of Cole's boot, tripping her. He reached out and grabbed her by the arm, stopping her fall, but the cookies kept going.

"Oh, no!" Tears welled in Maggie's eyes as she looked at the now upside-down tray on the floor. "I'm sorry. I didn't mean—"

Cole glared at Leland, waiting for the father he remembered to appear—the one who would tear down Maggie with his words and make her feel worthless.

"It's okay, sweetie." Rae stooped to pick up the tightly wrapped tray. Turning it over, she said, "See, they're just fine." She peeled back the plastic and held it out to his father. "Would you like one?"

"I'd rather have two." He winked then made his selections. "Y'all help yourselves."

While Cole breathed a sigh of relief, Maggie swiped the sleeve of her shirt over her eyes, removing any trace of tears.

Eyeing the door, Leland said, "My Doris should be back soon. She likes cookies, too."

Rae shifted the tray to the kids and waited for them to choose, her gaze seeking out Cole's. He'd warned her about his father living in the past so she wouldn't be surprised when he started talking about his wife and son.

Slumping onto the side of the bed, Cole simply nodded.

Cookie in hand, Maggie settled on the floor in front of the older man. "Who's Doris?" She took a bite, sending red-and-green sprinkles tumbling into her lap.

Meanwhile, Max sought out Cole, his wariness on full display. Leland was a man, after all. Cole lifted the boy into his lap.

"She's my wife," said Leland.

"Does she play the piano?"

"She sure does." Leland looked surprised. "How did you know?"

Maggie simply shrugged. "Because I play piano, too."

Both Cole and Rae chuckled. Maggie was so

proud. Discovering her hidden talent was the best thing that could have happened.

"You and Doris ought to get along just fine then."

"Do you have any kids?" Maggie was totally carrying the conversation.

"Sure do. I have a son. He's smart as a whip. Athletic, too. And oh, how he loves his mama."

Max slid out of Cole's lap. "Where is he now?"

In that moment, Leland looked completely lost. "I—I don't recall. I haven't seen him in years."

Cole stood, taken aback by his father's sudden change. The man usually talked about his son as though he'd just stepped out of the room. Now he was talking about years.

"What's his name?" Maggie was on her knees now.

"His name is Cole."

Maggie and Max both twisted to look at him.

"That's his name." Maggie pointed.

Leland shifted his seemingly knowing gaze to Cole, staring intently as though— After all this time, was it possible his father finally remembered him?

"No, he's too old to be my boy."

Just like that, the moment was over. Leland was back in his own world, where life was perfect and he adored his wife and son.

Cole tried to dismiss the disappointment sifting through him, though it was like trying to ignore the sun on a cloudless day. Why was it so important to him that his father recognize him? What purpose would it serve?

Before he could torment himself any further, Rae slipped her hand into his. A simple, wordless move that spoke volumes, letting him know she was there and that she cared. Outside of his mother and Tilly, he'd never had that kind of relationship with anyone. And given that they were family, this was completely different.

Rae was so vibrant, so full of life. She was the kind of woman who loved deeply, and those she loved were blessed to have her in their lives. What he wouldn't give to be one of them.

Because, despite everything he'd told himself, he was falling for her.

Chapter Twelve

Rae was getting used to having Cole around. No, it was more than that. She liked having him around, and actually looked forward to their time together, whether it was with the kids or just the two of them. He was open and honest, a calming presence in her often chaotic life, and he put others first, something Sean had never done. When they were married, everything had always been about him and his happiness. But Cole went out of his way to prove he had her back.

That made it kind of difficult to ignore the thrill that skittered through her when he'd drop by the café unexpectedly. She'd even started watching the clock, anticipating his visits right around ten each morning. Yes, whether she wanted to or not, she was falling for the handsome attorney who adored Maggie and Max every bit as much as she did.

That wasn't supposed to happen, though. Not only had she vowed never to marry again, she didn't want any romantic entanglements because they only led to heartache. Yet Cole made her want to forget all that. So where did she go from here?

While Johnny Mathis extolled the virtues of a winter wonderland, she sucked in a breath of sweetly scented air and looked at the two gingerbread houses on her kitchen table, along with all of the sprinkles, gumdrops and numerous other sugar-coma-inducing candies scattered around.

"I might need a chisel to remove all of this royal icing."

Cole grinned from the opposite side of the table where he was stacking Tootsie Roll logs outside the door of Max's house. "You did refer to it as glue."

"That was an understatement." She picked at a small blob with her fingernail. "This stuff is hard as a rock."

Her phone rang and she pulled it from her back pocket to see Christa's name. *Finally.*

She looked at Cole. "I need to take this. Are you okay for a couple of minutes?"

Without looking up, he said, "Sure."

"Great. Y'all keep working. I'll be back in a few." She hurried down the hall and outside. "Hello?"

"Sorry it took me so long to call you back."

"No problem." Rae rubbed her arms. The sun had barely set, yet the air was cooling fast.

"So what's up?"

"Have all of Dixie's puppies been spoken for?" While they wouldn't be ready to leave their mother for another week or so, Christa said she'd had several people reserving them already.

"Not yet. We still have four available. Two males, two females. Why? Are you thinking about getting one for the kids?"

She leaned against the door. "No way. We live in an apartment, remember?"

"You must be asking for someone else then."

"I want to give Cole a puppy for Christmas." Ever since he'd told her about his dog, Bo, she couldn't help thinking that a puppy might be therapeutic for him. He'd been alone for far too long.

"Oh. Cool." Rae could hear the underlying questions in Christa's vague response. "Does this mean—?"

"The only thing it means is that I want to give him something I think he would truly enjoy." If she wasn't willing to acknowledge her feelings for Cole to herself, there was no way she'd share her turmoil with anyone else.

"If you say so," said Christa. "But you know who you're talking to, right? I can tell when you're not owning up to your feelings." Sure she could. Because Christa had tried to ignore her feelings for Mick. Until Rae, Paisley and Laurel had set her straight.

Rae did not want to find herself in that position. Her friends were nothing if not relentless. "That's a discussion for another day. Can I purchase a puppy or not?"

"Yes. Male or female?"

"Male."

"All right, I've got you down."

"Thank you." She tucked her phone away and stared up at the starry sky, excitement tangling with half a dozen other emotions she'd never expected to feel after her divorce. *God, I don't want to be hurt again.*

Returning to the kitchen, she noted the time. After six already? And she had nothing planned for dinner. Looked like they were having frozen pizza.

"I finished my house." Maggie smiled proudly.

"That is so pretty." Rae moved beside her to take in the candy-coated confection dripping with frosting icicles and an abundance of red and green candies. "Very traditional, too.

I love it." She pulled out her camera. "Let's get a picture."

No sooner had she tucked her phone away again than Max announced he was done. His house was much simpler, adorned with mostly icing and marshmallows. But the peppermint path that led to the house along with the stacked "logs" beside the door gave it a nice rustic feel.

Again, she reached for her phone. "All right, Max. Give me a big smile."

Picture taken, she said, "Now we just need to let them dry and then we can display them in the living room."

"I want to eat mine." Max's smile was impish.

"After all that hard work?" Cole sent the boy an incredulous look.

"Let's enjoy them for a while." Rae moved to the stove. "How about pizza instead?"

"Pizza!" both kids cheered.

By the time she kissed Maggie and Max good-night, she was exhausted. And she still had to clean up the kitchen.

Cole was scrapping icing from the table with a spatula when she returned. "Man, you weren't kidding about this stuff."

"I should've covered the table." She eyed the two houses that now sat on the counter. "They sure had fun, though."

"I did, too."

She sensed Cole beside her and turned, her gaze colliding with his. "Perhaps I should have made a third house for you."

"Nah, Max and I learned together. Maybe I can do my own next time."

Next time? As in next Christmas?

Don't go there.

"Come on, I'll help you get this place cleaned up." He motioned to the decorated houses. "Where would you like me to put these?"

"Right there." She pointed to a small table in the living room, topped with batting snow.

While he did that, she moved to the sink and turned on the water. Seemed there were traces of icing on just about everything.

"Mmm...this stuff is pretty good." Cole came up beside her, holding a half-full bag of icing. He squeezed a small amount onto his finger then licked it off.

"Good thing I used powdered egg whites."

"Aw, don't tell me you've never eaten any."

"Not since I was ten, when my aunt Veronica shared the joys of salmonella with us kids."

He added another dollop to his finger. "But you said this has no raw eggs." His eyes held a mischievous glimmer.

The next thing she knew, that icing-topped finger was moving in her direction. "Don't you dare." In her attempt to evade his trickery, her cheek sideswiped the sticky white concoction. "Eww."

Before she could retaliate, a sound she'd never heard before had her looking Cole's way. He was laughing. A full-blown, doubled-over, gasping-for-air belly laugh. It may have been the sweetest sound she'd ever heard, and she couldn't help but laugh herself.

"I… I'm sorry." He sucked in a breath and straightened. "I'm not laughing at you."

"Yes, you are." She touched her now sticky cheek.

"Here—" he moved toward the sink "—let me get it." He grabbed a paper towel and dampened it before returning to her side. Cupping her chin in his hand, he said, "Hold still while I remove these hairs that are stuck." His touch was gentle, though it ignited a whirlwind of sensations inside her. "There we go." He moved the wet paper towel to her cheek. "You know, there's something I've been meaning to tell you."

Feeling his breath on her face, she swallowed hard. "Oh?"

Finished, he set the towel aside and looked at her. "Thank you for making me believe in Christmas." His smile was unlike any she'd seen before. Then she realized what was different—it had reached his eyes.

Her quick intake of breath was muffled by a tender kiss, filled with a longing rivaled only by her own. Her heart thundered in her chest as her hands moved up his arms and around his neck. No longer could she deny her feelings for this incredible man who'd unexpectedly captured her heart. He was everything she'd ever wanted in a man but never thought she'd find.

Suddenly he pulled away and stepped back, leaving her gasping for air.

His expression was a mixture of horror and confusion. "I shouldn't have done that."

Still trying to think straight, she said, "Why not? I mean...it was unexpected, but I—" She sucked in a breath. "I'm pretty sure this connection isn't one-sided." *Lord, please.*

"No, it's not." He shoved a hand through his hair. "This is my fault. I shouldn't have let things get away from me." He began to pace. "It's just that these past few weeks with you and the kids have been the best of my life. I've never felt more alive."

"I don't see how that's a problem."

"How can you not? I told you about my dad."

He wasn't making any sense. "What does that have to do with us?"

"It has everything to do with us. My father is the reason I've always avoided relationships."

"Cole, you said yourself, he's not the man you grew up watching."

"No, but his blood runs through my veins." Finally, he met her gaze, his own tormented. "I care about you, Rae. More than I dare to admit. But I'm not free to act on those feelings. I have to walk away."

"Walk away?" Her body stiffened. "Cole, whatever you're trying to tell me, I wish you'd just spit it out."

"I'm afraid of becoming like my father. And if I ever hurt you, I wouldn't be able to live with myself."

"You're too late then. Because you just did."

Cole drove across town Wednesday afternoon, asking himself for the umpteenth time why he'd kissed Rae. Things had been going so well between them. They were comfortable with each other. He'd had a connection with her he'd never had with anyone before. And then he'd ruined everything by kissing her.

He could still see the ache in her blue eyes, and knowing that he'd been the one to hurt her gutted him. The one thing he'd never wanted to do, had tried to avoid his whole life, he'd finally done. What he wouldn't give to go back to that playful moment and do it all over again, sans the kiss that had doomed the best friendship of his life. Now he couldn't even bear to look at Rae.

He pulled into the nursing home parking lot, killed the engine and grabbed the box of Moon-Pies from the passenger seat before exiting his truck. Gray blanketed the sky and a stout north wind had him hurrying inside the festive lobby. And to think, just a few days ago he'd been looking forward to spending Christmas with Rae and the kids. Now he couldn't wait for it to be over.

He continued into his father's hallway.

"Merry Christmas, Cole!" Mrs. Ida waved as he passed.

"You, too," was the only response he could muster.

The *Jeopardy* theme song echoed throughout the hallway as he continued to his father's room. How he wished the Leland of today had been the man who'd raised him. Maybe then Cole wouldn't be so messed up.

He knocked before entering, despite the door being open. "How's it going, Leland?" The man was in his wheelchair, looking a little out of sorts. Maybe the MoonPies would cheer him up.

"I brought you something." He passed the man the box.

"My favorite," his dad said. "Thank you." But instead of tearing into the box the way he usually did, he set it aside, clasped his hands in his lap and continued to stare at the floor.

Crouching, Cole rested a hand on the arm of the chair. "You feeling okay, Leland?"

"I'm a little tired today."

Trying to keep the conversation going, he said, "I guess Doris had to run out again?"

His father looked at him. "Who?"

That was different. "Doris. Your wife."

"Oh. Yeah. I reckon she had an errand to run." The man's gaze narrowed. "You doin' all right?"

No, he wasn't. But was it that obvious, even to a man who had no idea who he was? "I'll be fine." He pushed to his feet. "Though I suppose I ought to leave you alone so you can get some rest."

"I believe I could use a little nap."

"Would you like me to help you into bed?"

"That'd be mighty kind of you."

Once the man was settled, Cole said farewell then let the nurse know on his way out that his father was in bed.

He'd just passed the big Christmas tree and was approaching the exit when his phone rang. Pulling it from the breast pocket of his suit jacket, he saw Tilly's name on the screen. He was tempted not to answer. If his aunt picked up on his moroseness, she'd ask a thousand questions. Of course, if he didn't answer, she'd call until he did.

Pushing the door open, he hurried to his truck, willing an upbeat tone into his voice as he set the phone to his ear. "And how's my favorite aunt today?"

She chuckled. "Well, given that I'm your only aunt, the competition wasn't too tough."

He used the fob to unlock his truck and climbed inside, eager to be out of the wind. "It's kind of chilly down here. What kind of weather are you having up there in Waco?"

"It's cold. Rainy. And since when do you talk about the weather?"

"Just making small talk." He fired up the engine and turned on his seat warmer.

"You're not a small talk kind of guy, Cole. So do you want to go ahead and tell me what's bothering you or are you going to make me pry it out of you?"

"Hold on a sec while my phone connects to the truck so I'll be hands-free." Once it did, he backed out of his parking space, eager to change the subject. "What did you decide to do about Christmas? Are you going to stay there?" He moved the gearshift to Drive.

"Evasion tactics won't work. Yes, I've decided to stay. However, I'm not above coming back down there and hounding you until you tell me what's wrong."

"You're overreacting. I'm fine." Pulling out of the parking lot, he headed toward his house a few blocks away.

"Cole Heinsohn, don't you dare lie to me. Something has you troubled. I can hear it in your voice, so you may as well give it to me straight because you know I won't let you rest until you do."

Making a right turn, he heaved a sigh. "I'm just tired, that's all." Tired of hoping for the kind of life he could never have.

"I'm not buying that." She was quiet for a moment. "I spoke with Rae earlier today. She sounded about as miserable as you."

All because of him. He'd given her false hope by kissing her when he'd known a relationship with her would never be possible.

"That's too bad." He took a left.

"Yes, it is. And I don't think it's a coincidence that both of you are down in the dumps. Did something happen between the two of you?"

"The Mistletoe Ball is over."

Another pause. One that lingered until he pulled into his driveway.

"You like Rae, don't you? And I don't mean as a friend," Tilly was quick to add.

"What does it matter? You know where I stand on relationships."

"Yes, but sometimes the head forgets to tell the heart."

Lately, his heart seemed to have a mind of its own. "As Leland Heinsohn's son, that's not something I can afford."

His aunt was silent for a long moment before releasing an exasperated breath.

"Cole, I promised your mother I would never tell you this, but I'm afraid I'm going to have to pray that she'll forgive me because there's something you need to know."

He parked the vehicle and waited for her to continue.

"I'm guessing you don't remember, but your father used to be a kind, loving man and he was over the moon for your mother. Leland would have done anything for her."

Cole definitely had no recollection of that. "So, what happened?"

She drew in a breath. "Your parents were in a car accident when you were still quite young. Your father suffered a brain injury."

He straightened, eyeing his rearview mirror as his across-the-street neighbor's inflatable snowman came to life. "I don't remember any accident. Where was I?"

"Do you remember staying with Gary and me for a few days when you were three?"

"Vaguely."

"We were only supposed to have you for the night, while they went out to a party, but then your father was hospitalized. At first, he was fine, but months after the incident, Leland began to change. He became…short-tempered."

Cole's stomach clenched. "You mean he became abusive."

"Because of the injury, yes."

He'd always wondered how his mother could have fallen in love with someone who treated her like a piece of garbage. So at least he understood that now. Still. "He was so mean to her. To us. Why didn't she leave him?" Emotion clogged his throat. "She'd have been so much happier." And possibly might have still been with them today.

"Doris blamed herself for what happened."

"How could it be her fault?"

"Your father had had a few drinks, so she was the designated driver. They were on a country road, at night. A deer ran out in front of the car and she swerved to avoid it but ended up in the ditch. Your mother was fine, but your father wasn't wearing a seat belt and hit his head on the window. She was able to drive on out and get him to a hospital in the next county so no one in Bliss would know, but she never forgave herself. She simply looked at your father's treatment of her as penance."

Cole dragged a hand through his hair, feeling as though he might be sick. Why would his mother keep that from him? He'd been well into his forties when she passed and yet she'd never said a word. "Why didn't she want anyone to know?"

"She was ashamed."

"That doesn't make any sense. My father is the one who should have been ashamed. He ruined her life!"

"That's not how she viewed things. She knew she could've left. Contemplated it once. But she loved him. For better or worse."

"Love should not mean living in constant fear." He ground the words out. It had been a long time since he'd been this angry, and he'd never been upset with his mother before. But this? How could she just let him go on believing his father was innately abusive?

All those times Cole had tried to talk her into leaving—even long after he'd moved out of the house—she'd simply smile, pat him on the shoulder and say, "He's my husband," as if that made his father's treatment of her acceptable.

"She made her choice, Cole. I'm only telling you this now because I'm tired of seeing you living out your penance the way your mother did. Yes, in many ways, you are like your father. The way he used to be, back before the accident. Kind, tenderhearted, selfless...but Leland's abusive tendencies are not hereditary.

"Cole, I've always loved you as if you were my own son." Tilly was crying now. "And I've watched you walk this earth for nearly fifty years, but I have yet to see you truly live. You're simply going through the motions, afraid to get close to anyone. That's not how God intended any of us to live. Jesus came so that we could have abundant life." She sniffed. "I'm telling you the truth, because I want to see you step out of the darkness that has shrouded you all these years and embrace the life God has called you to. You are a good man who deserves to love and be loved."

Emotions warred inside him as tears wet his cheeks. Why hadn't his mother told him the truth? "I don't know if I can."

"Of course you can, dear. With God, *all* things are possible."

Chapter Thirteen

Wearing her maid of honor attire, a stylish black cocktail dress adorned with a red-satin sash, Rae stood at the windows of the bridal suite on the third floor of Renwick Castle, watching the river wind its way southward toward the Gulf of Mexico, wondering if Cole would be at the wedding. It had been almost a week since he'd walked out of her apartment for the last time. She'd never anticipated the gaping hole his absence would leave in her heart and her life. How was that even possible?

Naturally, Maggie and Max had noticed his absence, too. Every day they posed the same question. "Will we see Mr. Cole tonight?"

Funny, his earnest wish had been to be a positive influence in their lives. He'd definitely achieved that. And they missed him terribly.

On the opposite side of the room, Paisley sat

in front of an antique vanity, fixing her hair while Laurel and Christa joked and giggled like a couple of teenagers. Rae was happy for her friends, pleased they'd all found love. She'd never been envious of them for it until now. Rae had finally been given a glimpse of what they shared with their husbands, only to have the door slammed in her face.

Boy, was she feeling sorry for herself or what? Some maid of honor she was.

With a deep breath, she tore her gaze away from the window and joined her friends as Paisley stood. At five-foot-ten, the bride was a vision in her champagne-colored, lacy floor-length dress. Her beautiful red hair had been pinned back in the front while her long locks cascaded past her shoulders.

Looking at Rae, she asked, "Will you help me with my veil, darlin'?"

"You know I will." Since Paisley provided baked goods for the café every morning, she'd been the first to pick up on Rae's melancholia on Monday morning. And then grilled her until Rae opened up about all that had happened between her and Cole in recent weeks, though she'd kept Cole's family secret to herself. That information was not hers to share. Her friends knew her heartache and they would love her back to normal, no matter how long it took.

As Rae finished pinning the veil into place, there was a knock at the door.

A moment later, Paisley's mother entered. "Guests are arriving, so they'll be ready for you soon."

The wedding was set for five o'clock, followed by dinner and dancing, all of which would take place in the ballroom. Even one of the castle's owners would be in attendance, feeling as though she'd played a small role in bringing Paisley and Crockett together.

"All right—" Christa hugged them both "—we're going to join your families and ours. We'll see you soon."

Laurel hugged them, too. "See you in a bit."

After fussing over her daughter and shedding a few tears, Paisley's mother departed, in search of more tissues.

"Do you think Cole will come?" Paisley reached for Rae's hand. "We sent him an invitation."

"Between his tendency to be reclusive and the fact that I'm here, I don't expect to see him." No matter how much she might want to.

"Well, I'm going to keep praying that he'll show."

"It's okay. I'll be fine. I've got Maggie and Max." Who'd been with Wes all afternoon. "That's all I ever wanted."

"I know it is, darlin'. But cobbler is always better with a little ice cream."

Rae couldn't help laughing. "That is the weirdest analogy ever."

"Ah, but it's true."

Closing the gap between them, she hugged her friend. "I'm glad you and Crockett found each other."

"Me, too." Paisley took a step back. "Though it wasn't easy. So don't give up on Cole just yet."

She smiled, wishing it were that simple. But it was Cole who'd given up, sentencing himself to life that was anything but what God intended for those who loved Him.

A short time later, they made their way down the elevator to the ballroom that had been decorated to look like a wintry forest with snow-covered evergreen trees and boughs and thousands of tiny white lights. Approximately a hundred and fifty people were present to watch Paisley and Crockett exchange vows, none of which was Cole.

After dinner, Wes accompanied Rae onto the dance floor for the wedding party dance since Crockett's best man had been his father.

"You're looking pretty spiffy tonight, sis."

"Wes, do you want me to bop you upside the head like I did when we were kids? 'Spiffy' is how your Navy buddies look in their dress uniforms."

"Well, drop-dead gorgeous is reserved for my wife."

She hiked a brow. "That's all you've got, huh?"

"Sarah-Jane is cute."

"She's a toddler." Her brother had a habit of driving her to the point of exasperation.

He twirled her once before reeling her back to him. "I guess that makes you beautiful, then." His teasing smile had her insides going all soft and mushy.

"You pulled that one out of your hat just in the nick of time, didn't you?"

"Yeah, but it's the truth. You are beautiful. Always have been."

She felt her cheeks heating. "Thank you."

"Though you're not your usual bubbly self." Blue eyes so reminiscent of Sarah-Jane's narrowed on her. "That wouldn't have anything to do with Cole, would it?"

"Has Laurel not said anything to you?" She would've thought the topic of her and Cole would be a major talking point.

"Obviously she's been holding out on me. I thought things were going well between you and Cole."

"They were."

"But?"

There was no way she was going into detail at her best friend's wedding. "It's complicated."

"Could it be that what happened with Sean is holding you back?"

Her brother knew her too well. "Cole has some baggage, too."

"Laurel and I know all about that." He cast her a very matter-of-fact look. "So do Crockett and Paisley and Mick and Christa."

Sorrow welled inside her. "At this point, it doesn't really matter." Only God could free Cole from his past. "There's nothing I can do."

"If you care about him, don't give up, Rae. Where there's love, there's hope."

Her gaze shot to his. "Who said anything about love?"

"You didn't have to." Wes smiled, obviously pleased with his deduction, no matter how misguided it might be. "Cole is a good man. He's been good for you."

"What makes you—?" Just then, she saw Cole enter the ballroom. Maggie and Max saw him, too. They hurried in his direction, making him smile. But there was definitely a sad air about him.

"He's here," she whispered to Wes. "I didn't think he'd come. He wasn't here for the ceremony."

"Maybe he's here for the cake."

Lips pursed, she glared at her brother.

"Or perhaps he came because he knew you'd be here." Wes released his hold on her as the song ended.

"I'm nervous."

"Come on, Rae. What's the worst thing that could happen?"

She supposed he had a point. Since Cole had already made it clear he couldn't be with her, things couldn't get any worse. That didn't stop her insides from fluttering, though.

Wes escorted her off the dance floor as another slow country tune began. Leaning toward her, he said, "If nothing else, you're still friends, so just act natural."

As if *that* was going to happen. Not after that amazing kiss. One that had ended all too abruptly.

Out of the corner of her eye, she saw Cole moving toward her with Maggie and Max in tow.

"Mama Rae, Mr. Cole's here," said Max.

"I see that." She looked at him, hoping he couldn't see how edgy she felt. "I'm glad you could make it."

"Me, too." His gaze skimmed over her. "You look beautiful."

Why did she find herself hoping for drop-dead gorgeous? "Thank you."

He looked from Maggie to Max. "Would it be all right with you two if I dance with your mother?"

Maggie nodded emphatically while Max made the same face he gave when presented with broccoli.

Cole took hold of her hand and led her onto the floor. When his arm moved around her waist, she couldn't help thinking about that kiss and wondering if he'd dwelled on it as much as she had.

"I didn't see you earlier," she finally said.

"I just got here. I wasn't planning to come but..." His gaze met hers. "I wanted to see you."

Her hopes soared. *Lord, please don't let them crash and burn.*

"About Sunday night. I never meant to hurt you. Yet that's exactly what I did. I'm sorry."

All she could do was stare.

"I talked to Tilly this week." He briefly looked away.

"Is she going to stay in Waco for Christmas?" She hated this small talk.

"Yes. She...also told me some things about my father I never knew."

Curious, Rae said, "What kind of things?"

Before he could respond, his phone vibrated in his breast pocket. With a sigh, he pulled it out. "It's the nursing home. I have to take it."

"Yes, of course." She followed him off the dance floor, through the maze of beautifully decorated tables and into the hall.

"Hello?" He paused, his brow furrowing, his expression intense. "I'm on my way." Ending the call, he said, "My father had a heart attack. Ambulance is taking him to the hospital."

She followed him to the stairs. "Would you like me to go with you?"

"Thank you, but no. You stay and enjoy your friends." He was midway down the steps when he turned back. "Will you do me a favor, though?"

"Anything."

"Pray."

Concern for his father nearly overwhelmed Cole as he drove through the streets of Bliss, pushing the boundaries of the speed limit. It had been three days since Tilly had shared the truth behind his father's behavior and Cole still couldn't understand why his mother had never told him about the man's injury. If she had, it might have changed how he regarded his father. Instead of seeing him as a monster, Cole might have been able to view the man with a little more compassion. He could have researched his father's condition to see if there were any treatments. Or had his mother done that and been left empty-handed?

Cole would never know how those missing pieces of his life might have changed things. Not that any of that mattered right now. He simply needed to get to his father. And the faster, the better.

His grip tightened on the steering wheel. *God, please don't call my father home before I get there. There's so much I need to say to him.*

He whipped into the hospital parking lot, continued around to the emergency entrance and pulled into the first available space. His hands shook as he turned off the ignition. Under an inky sky, he hastily exited the vehicle and jogged through the cool night air to the sliding doors.

Crossing the tiny waiting room to the check-in window, he scanned the nurses' station on the other side, looking for someone to call out to, but it was empty. Were they all with his father? At least that would mean he was still alive.

He took a step back, noting the call button next to the window. He pressed it multiple times, not caring if it annoyed anyone. He needed to know what was happening with his father.

Finally, a young woman in floral scrubs approached, her lips pressed tightly together. She slid the window aside. "Can I help you?"

"I'm here for Leland Heinsohn." The words rushed out. "They brought him via ambulance."

"Are you related?" As if anyone else would be here.

"He's my father."

"They're working on him now. I'll let the doctor know you're here." With that, she closed the window, turned her back and walked away, leaving Cole to wonder and worry.

He paced the recently polished floor, from the snack and soda machine to the uncomfortable-looking green chairs on the opposite wall, and back again. The space was so small, though, that he soon felt dizzy.

Dropping into a chair that allowed him to see what was going on behind the narrow stretch of glass, he leaned his head against the wall as thoughts of Rae drifted through his mind. She'd looked so beautiful the night of the Mistletoe Ball, but that paled in comparison to her appearance tonight. Whether it was the dress or the hair, he couldn't be certain, but she was downright gorgeous. Looking into her blue eyes while he'd held her in his arms had felt like coming home after a long, arduous journey. Only, his journey wasn't over. And he wasn't sure he'd ever be able to live a life free of his past—the kind of life other people took for granted.

Just when he was entertaining the notion of pressing the buzzer again, he saw movement on the other side of the glass. Moments later, the door opened and Reid Spencer, another Bliss native, though several years younger than Cole, emerged wearing blue scrubs. Like Cole, he'd gone away to college, then medical school as opposed to Cole's law school, before returning to serve the people of Bliss.

Cole shot to his feet. "How is he?"

"At the moment, he's stable. We're going to transport him to Austin Heart as soon as the helicopter can get here."

Helicopter? This was no minor heart attack. At least he could take comfort in knowing that Austin Heart was one of the best in the state. But it was a good hour and a half to two hours away, depending on traffic. What if something happened before Cole could get there?

"Can I see him?"

Reid nodded. "I'll take you back." He motioned for Cole to follow, leading him past a series of desks with monitors. Antiseptic smells filled the air as they rounded a corner to a triage room that was three times the size of the waiting room.

Inside, his dad lay atop a narrow gurney, his eyes closed. A white blanket was draped over his torso while tubes and wires extended from various parts of his body. And his chest rose and fell at an erratic pace.

"I'll be close by, if you need me," said Reid.

"Thank you." Cole moved tentatively into the sterile room. The man who'd once been a towering, robust rancher now lay weak and pale.

Cole inched closer, his gaze drifting to the jagged line on the heart monitor. Jagged was good. It meant his father was still alive.

"My. Boy."

Cole started at his father's raspy voice. He looked down to discover Leland's eyes open and fixed on Cole.

"I thought…you'd never come." His father struggled for each breath.

Emotion thickened Cole's throat and he blinked back tears. Did the man really know who he was?

"Of course I came. You're my father and I… I love you."

"Love you." The man drew in a ragged breath. "Son."

Cole gulped for air, looking away as a small sob escaped. It was true. His father recognized him.

He reached for the frail, veiny hand resting atop the blanket and gave it a gentle squeeze, sending tears trailing from the corners of the man's eyes.

"Can you... Forgive. Me?" Leland took a breath and pressed on. "What I did... You. Mother. Loved. Both. Much."

Cole closed his eyes, ignoring the wetness soaking his cheeks. His father remembered him. Remembered everything.

Finally finding his voice again, he stared down at the man he'd never had the opportunity to truly see until now. "I know you did, Dad."

Confused eyes so like his own stared up at him. "You...do?"

He nodded, feeling himself smile. "It's okay. It wasn't your fault." He sniffed. "Of course I forgive you."

The man smiled back and closed his eyes. Cole had never seen him look so serene. The torment that had plagued his father for so much of his life had finally ceased. The battle that no doubt raged inside him was over.

Soon, his hand went limp and slipped from Cole's grasp as the beeping of the heart monitor went from incremental to one long, steady sound, and hospital staff rushed into the room. Cole wasn't concerned, though, because for the first time in a very long while, his father was at peace. The past was behind him.

If only Cole could let go of his.

Chapter Fourteen

Cole poured another cup of coffee in his kitchen late the next morning, still numb from last night.

After leaving the hospital, he'd gone to the farmhouse, wanting—make that *needing*—to see if he felt any different about the place, looking at it through the lens of truth. He couldn't say it had been a pleasant experience, but he hadn't felt the need to bolt from the house the way he usually did, either.

It had been somewhere close to three this morning when he'd returned to his place. Yet, while he'd been exhausted, sleep had eluded him. His mind raced with the things Tilly had said, his father's final words, and the funeral Cole now had to plan, leaving him feeling completely overwhelmed. He wasn't even going to have a funeral, but Tilly had insisted, saying it's what his mother would have wanted. She was probably right, though he doubted anyone would come.

Now Tilly was on her way back to Bliss to accompany him to the funeral home for the arrangements. He had yet to mention anything to her about that last conversation with his father, though. That was something that needed to be done in person.

As he sipped his fourth cup of the morning, he eyed the red-and-green candy cane ornament Max had made for him, dangling from the knob on the cupboard. It was the only Christmas decoration in his house. Much different from Rae's, where there was something festive everywhere you looked.

He felt a sad smile tug at the corners of his mouth. It seemed Rae was never far from his thoughts. Had the wedding really been just last night? It felt like forever since he'd held her in his arms, longing to tell her what he'd learned from Tilly. He'd thought it would be easier to share the information in a public place rather than in the intimacy of her cozy apartment where he'd be tempted to believe that the life he'd dared to dream of was finally within his reach.

So much for the truth setting him free. He wasn't sure he'd ever be free. Yes, he felt good about having closure with his father, but moving forward with the kind of relationship he longed to have with Rae still made him uneasy. Because, while the chains of his past may have been broken, he was still dragging them around. It was exhausting to say the least, but they'd been a part of him for so long he didn't know anything else.

The doorbell rang and he eyed the clock on his microwave. Eleven thirty. He'd texted Tilly to let her know their appointment wasn't until one thirty. Knowing his aunt, though, she was probably worried and had come early to dote on him. She really was like a second mother to him.

Rounding the granite-topped island, he continued across the tiled floor in his bare feet, into the entry hall and to the front door. When he pulled it open, his heart all but stopped. It wasn't Tilly who stood there. It was Rae.

"Hi," was all he could manage to say.

She held a paper bag. "I heard about your father at church this morning. I'm so sorry."

"I should have let you know, but I—"

"That's all right. I'm sure you have a lot on your mind."

Did she realize she was one of those things?

"I just wanted to drop off some food. I'm sure you'll be receiving lots of it, but I brought your favorite. At least, I *think* it's your favorite."

"Please tell me it's chicken and dumplings."

"You mean chicken dumplings?" Her smile nearly undid him.

"How could I forget?" Max had woven his way into Cole's heart right along with Maggie. But it was Rae who'd showed him how good life could be. If he were someone else.

"There should be enough for a couple of meals." She held out the bag.

"Would you like to come in?" He knew he should just accept the bag and let her go on her way but, aside from Tilly, she was the only person who knew the secrets he harbored. "I have something I'd like to share with you."

"All right." She stepped into the foyer and he noticed her gaze darting around the space. Only then did he realize that she'd never been inside his house before.

He led her into the kitchen where he promptly unpacked the bag, discovering cookies in a third container. "Thank you." After tucking the soup in the refrigerator, he looked her way. "Would you care for a cup of coffee?"

She paused on the other side of the island, seemingly nervous. "Yeah, that'd be good. It's pretty chilly out there today."

"Where are the kids?" He grabbed a cup and filled it.

"They went home with Wes and Laurel."

After setting the cup in front of her, he retrieved the creamer from the fridge. "I don't have time to go into a lot of detail. Tilly will be in soon. We have a meeting at the funeral home to make the arrangements."

"When is the funeral?" She lifted the lid on the creamer and poured.

"Tuesday. I wanted Tilly to be able to head back to Waco for Christmas without feeling rushed." He moved around the island, pulled out a stool and sat. "I found out some things this week that were...well, pretty shocking."

"About?" She blew across the top of her drink.

"My father." He rubbed his chin, noting that he still had to shave. "Tilly shared a deep, dark secret with me that my mother took to her grave."

Rae listened intently as he told her about the injury that had caused the change in his father and his mother's determination to keep it to herself.

"Wow." She gripped her mug. "That's...well, on the one hand, I admire her for wanting to protect your father and to honor her marriage vows, but on the other hand, I don't understand why she wouldn't tell you. It might have helped you see your father in a different light."

"I thought the same thing." He wanted to tell

her about what happened at the hospital, but he wasn't sure he could get through it without breaking down.

"So, at the hospital… Was your father unconscious the whole time or were you able to speak with him?"

So much for holding back. When he hesitated, though, she set a hand to his arm. "It's okay. You don't have to tell me." The warmth in her fingers seeped into his skin.

"Actually, something quite remarkable happened." He looked at her. "For the first time in a very long while, he was in his right mind. He knew who I was. And he asked my forgiveness."

"Cole, that's wonderful. How sweet of God to allow you both that closure."

"You'd think, but there's still so much in here, Rae." He pounded his fist against his chest. "All my life I've felt like an outsider, watching other people live their lives while I've been held captive by my past. Yes, I should be able to move on, but I can't. When Tilly told me about my father, she assured me his issues weren't hereditary, that I was free from the worries that plagued me. But I can't seem to let go of this long-held fear that I'll hurt someone. It's like it's a part of me."

"Only if you allow it to be."

"I don't know how not to."

He stood then and moved to the closet beside the front door, ready to change the subject. He retrieved a large shopping bag and, returning to the kitchen, he handed it to her. "Here are the gifts I bought for the kids."

She looked from the bag to him, pain visible in her pretty eyes. Pain he'd caused. Again. "Wouldn't you prefer to give them to Maggie and Max yourself?"

"More than anything. I just don't think I can, though."

Her expression morphed from hurt to anger just as the doorbell rang.

"That would be Tilly." He was grateful for the reprieve because it was killing him to look at Rae.

She pushed her cup aside, grabbed the bag and followed him to the door. He opened it.

"My dear—" Tilly simply stared, blinking, a hint of a smile on her pink lips. "Rae, I'm so glad you're here."

"I was just leaving." She whisked past his aunt and hurried to her SUV parked at the curb.

His heart ached as he watched her go. How different things could be if he truly were free. But he knew better than to hope.

"What was that all about?" Tilly stepped inside and he closed the door behind her.

"Long story."

"Good thing I came early then." She shrugged out of her jacket. "Pour me a cup of coffee and let's chat."

An hour later, they were still on the sofa, coffee cups long empty as he finished telling her about the events at the hospital.

"I—I'm stunned." Tilly grabbed another tissue from the box that sat between them. "Only God could have orchestrated something so amazing. That's the greatest gift you could have received."

"Gift?" He sent her an incredulous look. "I mean, the part about him knowing me was good. I'd been wanting that for a while. I hated pretending to be someone else when I was with him. Even when he was happy, he couldn't accept me for who I was."

His aunt shook her head, her gaze boring into him like never before. "Cole, you are so blind that you can't see the truth when it's right in front of you."

"What are you talking about?"

"The man you witnessed at the hospital wasn't the Leland Heinsohn who suffered from dementia or the angry monster you grew up knowing. That was your dad! The man who cradled you in his arms and sang you to sleep when you had colic. The one who protected you from the monster you thought lived in your closet. The one who loved you and your mother for as long as he was able, and the one whose blood runs through your veins. Cole, you *are* free."

He pushed to his feet and began to pace. "Then why do I still feel as though I'm chained to my past?"

She was beside him in an instant, a hint of a smile playing at her lips as she looked up at him. "Sometimes God removes our chains. Other times, He waits for us to give them to Him." She squeezed his arm. "Let go of your burden, Cole. It's not yours to carry."

A battle raged inside him—the past he'd believed warring with the future he longed to embrace. "How do I do that?"

"Jesus said, 'Come unto me, all ye that labor and are heavy laden, and I will give you rest.' Cole, with God, nothing is impossible. You only have to trust Him, just the way you did when you were a little boy and you trusted Him with your heart. You know the truth now. It's time you started walking in it."

Rae sucked in a breath of cool December air and walked into the funeral home Tuesday afternoon, because, try as she might, she couldn't *not* go to Cole's father's funeral, no matter how much Cole tried to push her away.

When she'd left his house on Sunday, she'd been angry. But only a small part of it had had to do with his backing out of Christmas. No, she was upset that this wonderful man was allowing himself to be eaten alive by his fears instead of handing them over to God.

And to make matters worse, she was in love with him.

Yes, even before she arrived at his place, she'd known she loved him. Late Saturday night, after returning to her apartment, she was praying for Cole and his father when the realization hit her. Despite vowing she'd never fall in love again, she'd gone and done just that with a man who was emotionally unavailable. Because while she'd had her heart broken, Cole's had been shredded over and over again.

Half a dozen people waited in the funeral home lobby that felt more like someone's living room with its plush carpet and comfortable furniture. Tilly chatted with a couple of them while the others waited to sign the guest book.

Rae knew the moment Tilly spotted her. She excused herself and headed in Rae's direction, clad in black leggings and a flowing black tunic, her arms wide.

"My dear, it's so good to see you."

Rae found herself welcoming the hug. "You, too. I just wish it were under different circumstances."

"I know." Tilly released her. "How are you doing?"

Rae sucked in a breath. "Good. Just busy, trying to make sure everything is perfect for Christmas."

"I'm sure Maggie and Max are excited."

"Oh, yes. They've already started the whole can-we-open-just-one-present thing. Of course, there are no presents under the tree yet, so that makes it easier to refuse them."

The older woman chuckled. "I remember when my girls were little. They were the same way." She sobered then, taking hold of Rae's hands. "But how are you, dear? I mean in here." She pointed to her heart. "Cole filled me in on everything that's happened between the two of you."

Everything? Rae couldn't help wondering what tools or tactics Tilly had had to use to get him to open up. But she was quite good at that. It seemed no one could refuse Tilly.

"I'm—" She started to say "fine," but knew her friend would see right through her. "I care for Cole very much, but he's a tortured man. And until he can allow God to heal him, there's no room in his life for me or anyone else."

"You're a very pragmatic young lady. But I know you're hurting, too."

Rae lifted a shoulder. "I'm a survivor. God has brought me through a lot in the course of my life and He'll bring me through this, too. Besides, I have Maggie and Max to keep me busy."

The door opened again, ushering in a burst of cold air along with an older couple.

Rae looked from them to Tilly. "I'm going to go find a seat."

After signing the guest book, she moved into another room that looked more like a church, with pews on both sides of a center aisle. Instrumental hymns echoed softly from overhead speakers while several flower arrangements delicately scented the space.

As she started down the aisle, her attention was drawn to the flower-draped casket at the front. Then she saw Cole sitting in the front pew all by himself. His elbows were on his knees, head down, as if he might be praying. Or hiding, hoping no one would talk to him.

She blinked back the tears that suddenly blurred her vision. How she wanted to march up there and sit beside him, letting him know she was there. But that wasn't her place.

Looking away, she noticed Mick and Christa several pews back and started toward them.

"What are you two doing here?" She kept her voice low.

Christa lifted a brow. "Do you really need to ask?"

Rae shook her head. "I mean, why?"

With one arm around his wife, Mick leaned closer. "Cole and I went to school together," he whispered. "Not to mention he helped me fight to keep Sadie."

Rae set her purse on the floor, her gaze again drifting to Cole. He was sitting up now, his focus straight ahead. She couldn't help wondering what was going on inside him. He shouldn't be up there alone. Why wasn't Tilly with him?

"Hey, y'all."

Rae looked up to see Paisley and Crockett moving into the pew.

Once her friend settled to her left, Rae leaned closer. "Shouldn't you two still be on your honeymoon?" She knew they'd planned just a short one at a resort out in the hill country, but still.

"We got back this morning," said Paisley. "Of course, we learned about the funeral on social media."

Her husband leaned in then. "Cole was instrumental in negotiating our contract with the Renwicks. He made sure we weren't going to be taken advantage of."

Again, Rae's eyes wandered to the front to

find Cole still alone. He turned his head ever so slightly. His forlorn expression tore at her heart. She hated to see him hurting.

Out of the corner of her eye, she saw Wes and Laurel squeeze into the end of the pew. She didn't need to ask why they were there. She was well aware of all the work Cole had done for both Wes and Laurel's father, Jimmy. And when she'd spoken with her sister-in-law earlier, she'd said that Jimmy would be keeping the kids.

So rather than worry about them, she continued to fret over the man everyone respected. Cole wasn't an outsider looking in on other people's lives; *he* was the one on the inside, refusing to let people in. And there was no way she was going to let him go through this alone.

Standing, she excused herself then scooted past Christa and Mick into the aisle. Only then did she notice how many people were in attendance. The place wasn't packed, and she had no idea how many of them had known Cole's father, but she had a sneaking suspicion that most of them were there for the same person her friends were. They knew and respected Cole. And whether he realized it or not, he was a vital part of this community.

Squaring her shoulders, she walked up the

aisle to the front row, sat next to Cole and reached for his hand.

His startled gaze moved from her face to their joined hands and back. Then he smiled ever so slightly. Yet despite the lack of oomph in his smile, there was a light in his eyes. One she'd never seen before, not even that night he'd kissed her. As they shifted from a silver-gray to a brilliant silver, her heart all but stopped.

The turmoil she was used to seeing was gone, replaced by a glorious, beautiful peace that went far beyond human understanding. God was on the move, working in Cole's life, drawing him out of the darkness and bringing him into the light of truth.

Tears filled her eyes. Cole deserved to be free. It didn't matter if he ever loved her or not; just knowing he'd been released from his past was enough.

God, thank You. Seeing Cole like this is the greatest gift I could have received this Christmas. And while You know the desires of my heart, if they don't align with Your will, I will rejoice in knowing that Cole is now free to live the life You've called him to.

Pastor Kleinschmidt approached and shook Cole's hand before settling on the opposite side of him. Cole was in good hands. He didn't need her anymore.

Without another word, she released his hand and returned to her seat. Cole would be fine. And though it might take some time, the ache in her heart would subside. For now, she would look forward to sharing Christmas with Maggie and Max—a Christmas they would always remember. Though without Cole, it wouldn't be as perfect as she'd once dreamed.

Chapter Fifteen

Cole leaned back in his office chair late Wednesday night and dragged a hand over his face, the past few days a blur in his groggy mind. With funeral plans set, he'd gone to Loving Hearts on Monday morning to clear out his father's belongings—a television, the recliner, clothes and a few mementos and personal effects, including a photo of his parents with a two-year-old Cole. His dad was holding him, his smile wide. Cole had never given the picture much thought before, but now that he knew about the accident that had changed his father and realized the snapshot had been taken before then, it had suddenly become very precious to him.

After dropping the items at the farmhouse, he'd met with Pastor Kleinschmidt, not only to discuss the funeral service but Cole's life and the recent revelations that had left him not only confused but uncertain of how to move forward. He would be eternally grateful to the man for patiently walking him through the scriptures, showing Cole how, time and again, God took people and situations that seemed hopeless and used them for good.

By the time he left the pastor's office hours after arriving, Cole felt a lightness about him that had never been there before. God was good, gracious, and far bigger than any of the things Cole had allowed control over his life. For the first time since he'd been a little boy, Cole had hope and he dared to dream of a future. Perhaps one with a beautiful blue-eyed brunette.

When Rae had come alongside him and taken his hand yesterday, he was reminded why it had been so difficult to fight his feelings for her. Rae put others before herself and stood up for the underdog. She was kind, giving, and did everything she could to make life a little better for those around her, whether it was a customer in the café, two little kids who'd been traumatized, or a lifeless attorney who'd never known the meaning of joy.

Yes, he loved Rae, and he couldn't wait to tell her, but the stack of papers waiting on his desk when he came into the office this morning had him putting his own desires on hold for at least one more day. Seemed everyone was trying to clear their desks before the holidays, leaving him numerous items to follow up on.

He reached for his travel mug and took a sip of lukewarm coffee, then noticed it was past 11:00 p.m. There was no way he was going to accomplish any more tonight. He may as well get a good night's rest and finish up in the morning. Tomorrow was Christmas Eve, so Brenda would be off, and he could work without interruption. Then he'd go to Rae, tell her how he felt, and pray she would still let him celebrate Christmas with her and the kids.

Grabbing his briefcase and suit jacket, he yawned as he headed for the back door. He stepped into the chilly night air and locked the door behind him. A few minutes later, he pulled his truck out of the alley, thankful for seat warmers.

He turned onto the side street then made a left onto Main, eyeing the front of his office as he slowly passed. A few doors down, his gaze shifted to the windows over the café. No lights there, either. Rae and the kids had probably been in bed for hours.

Turning his attention to the café below, he noticed it was also dark, save for a light at the back. Rae must've forgotten to flip the switch in the kitchen.

As he approached the corner, something niggled at his brain, raising the hairs on the back of his neck. He stopped, put his truck into Reverse and backed up. Again, he looked at the café, unable to shake the feeling that something wasn't right.

He parked, hopped out of his truck and hurried across the street. Nearing the picture window, he saw the light flicker and shift. He pressed his face to the glass, his gut clenching. That wasn't a light. While Rae and the kids were asleep upstairs, the café was on fire.

Heart thundering in his chest, he retrieved his phone from the pocket of his slacks and dialed 9-1-1.

"Nine-one-one, what is your—?"

"There's a fire at Rae's Fresh Start Café on Main Street. She and two children are asleep upstairs." Knowing that time was of the essence, particularly when one was dealing with a volunteer fire department, Cole ended the call, well aware that he couldn't wait for Rae and the kids to be rescued. He had to get them out now.

He dialed Rae's phone, on the off chance she might answer, all the while assessing the front of the building, determining how to get in. At least the back door had a bell. But he'd have to walk to the end of the block and around the buildings to get there, costing him precious time.

He tried the café door as his call went to voice mail. Locked, of course.

God, show me a way in.

Redialing, only one thing came to mind.

He looked around for something to break the window. By the time Rae's sweet voice told him to leave a message, he decided his only option was one of two large potted plants flanking the door of the café.

After tucking the phone away, he hoisted the pot into his arms, stepped back a few feet and propelled it through the window to the right of the door. The sound of shattering glass pierced the stillness of the night. When the ruckus finally settled, he kicked at a few jagged pieces sticking up from the frame before launching himself into the building.

The smell of smoke had him tucking his nose and mouth into the crook of his arm as he hurried through the maze of tables and chairs. He'd just made it to the stairs at the back of the dining room when the fire erupted behind him with a loud roar.

He stumbled into the wall. Grabbing hold of the railing, he continued to climb, the smoke growing thicker with each step. He could feel the heat intensifying at his back.

Reaching the landing at the top, he beat his fist against the wooden door. "Rae!" He coughed. "Wake up!" He pounded harder. Covering his nose and mouth again, he tried to take a deep breath, but choked. "Rae!" He banged again, struggling for a breath.

He took a step back and attempted to kick the door open. Once. Twice. *Come on, Rae.*

What if the smoke was already in the apartment? How long might she and the kids have been inhaling it as they'd slept? If they were unconscious, they'd never hear him.

He had to get them out.

His eyes burned as he frantically kicked and banged. He thrust his entire weight against the door.

God, help me!

"Rae!" He leaned his head against the door as coughs racked his body. If they didn't make it out, he'd never get the chance to tell her he loved her.

Suddenly the door opened.

He stumbled inside, bumping into a half-asleep Rae.

"Cole, what are you—?"

"Fire!" He coughed and tossed the door shut behind him before dashing to the kids' room.

"You have to get out of here." He heard Rae cough behind him as he pushed open the kids' bedroom door. "Can you get Max?" He was the lighter of the two.

Rae nodded, her eyes wide with fear.

They scooped the kids up, blankets and all, and hurried to the outside door. He twisted the dead bolt and thrust it open, sucking in a breath of fresh air. Rae snagged her keys from a hook beside the door on her way out then hurried down the back steps while Cole closed the door tightly.

When he joined her at her SUV, her blue eyes filled with tears and he saw trepidation behind them.

Her bottom lip trembled. "I'm afraid."

He wrapped an arm around her and kissed the top of her head, thanking God for getting them out safely. "You and the kids are safe. That's all that matters." And just as soon as Cole had the opportunity, he was going to tell her everything that was in his heart—including how much he loved her.

Cole had barely brought her SUV to a stop in front of the square when a cacophony of sirens ground to a halt in front of the café. Rae peered out the window as the firemen set to work, but not before she saw dark smoke billowing from both the front and back of the café and flames lapping at the edges of a broken window.

As she emerged from the vehicle, Johanna Dewitt, an EMT who was also a regular at the diner, hurried toward her, insisting she, Cole and the kids get checked out in the ambulance. Now, here she sat on a gurney, holding tightly to the blanket the EMT had wrapped around her as fear, uncertainty and more gratitude than she'd ever felt tangled into one overwhelming emotion. Cole was right, though—they were safe. And all because of him.

Her gaze drifted to the opposite side of the vehicle, to where he sat with Max at his side, an oxygen mask covering his nose and mouth. If it hadn't been for Cole, she and the kids likely wouldn't be sitting there now. He'd risked his life to save them.

Greater love hath no man—no, she wasn't going to go there.

She squeezed Maggie tighter, a part of her eager to step outside to see how her business had fared, while another part of her was afraid to know how bad it might be. But from what little she'd seen, she didn't hold out much hope.

How could this have happened? She was always so careful when she closed for the day. Had she been so distracted by her last-minute

Christmas preparations that she'd left something on? The stove? The deep fryer?

Not that it really mattered. At least, not right now. Maggie and Max were her main focus. They needed her. Needed to be assured that everything was going to be all right. They'd been traumatized enough in their young lives.

"I'm fine." Cole removed the plastic mask, much to Johanna's chagrin. While Rae and the kids had suffered very little smoke inhalation, Cole had taken in much more. Rae was in awe of the lengths he'd gone to, determined to make sure she and the kids were safe. Like a hero in one of those romance movies, risking life and limb to save the woman he loved. Not that Cole loved her. Still, he did care deeply, and that made him a hero in her book.

Johanna frowned at him. "With all due respect, sir, I'll be the judge of that." She eyed the oximeter attached to his finger before glaring back at him. "You're barely there. But given that you were the hero tonight, I suppose I can let you go." Taking the mask from Cole, she winked at Rae. "Can I interest you kids in a candy cane?"

Both Maggie and Max straightened, a light returning to their dark eyes.

"Yes, please," they said in unison.

Cole and Rae stepped out of the ambulance

into the cold night air before taking Maggie and Max into their arms.

"C'mon." Cole nodded toward his truck just a few feet away.

Rae followed him, her attention drifting to the café where white smoke now streamed from the building, indicating the fire was either out or almost out.

They placed the kids into the back seat then Cole hopped into the driver's seat to start the engine. As Rae closed the door, she noticed Paul Dorsey, the fire chief, moving in their direction. She returned to the driver's side, motioning for Cole to roll his window down.

"Do you mind staying with the kids while I talk to the fire chief?"

Glancing in his side mirror, he said, "Not at all."

She pulled her blanket tighter as she approached the back of the pickup. "Give it to me straight, Paul. How bad is it?"

"Not as bad as it could have been." He tilted his helmet back a notch. "Whoever called this in did so just in the nick of time. And the fact that you're standing here talking to me means they went to great lengths to make sure you and those children of yours got out alive."

Alive. The word made her shudder. "Any idea what caused it?"

He shook his head. "We won't know the cause or the full extent of damage for a while. All we've been able to narrow down so far is that it started in the kitchen."

Just as she suspected. But was it her fault?

"I hate to say this, Rae, with it being Christmas and all, but you're going to have to find another place to stay for a while."

The words slammed into her with force she hadn't expected. "Where are we supposed to go?"

"You'll stay at the farmhouse."

She whirled to find Cole standing behind her.

"Chief?" someone hollered behind him.

"If you'll excuse me," said Paul.

Looking up into Cole's caring eyes, Rae felt herself unraveling. Her home, her livelihood, her perfect Christmas…everything was gone. "All of the gifts." Her bottom lip trembled. "They were in the kitchen." She gulped for air. "I've got nothing."

His strong arms came around her then and he pulled her close as the tears she'd been fighting all night finally fell.

"Yes, you do," she heard him whisper. "You and Maggie and Max are safe, and you all are far more precious than anything that could come from a store. The three of you are the greatest gift of all."

She fisted the lapels of his suit coat and continued to sob, knowing he was right but still heartbroken that she wouldn't be able to give Maggie and Max the Christmas they deserved. The Christmas she longed to give them. Now their only memories would be of having to leave home—again.

Cole stroked her hair. "There's nothing more we can do here, so why don't we take the kids on out to the farmhouse."

She sniffed and pulled away, nodding. "They like it there." Unlike Cole. Yet he was willing to go there for her and the kids. She looked up at this wonderful man who'd done so much for her and Maggie and Max. And she'd thought the play area was expensive. Now he'd saved their lives, and that was absolutely priceless.

Smiling, she wiped away her tears, knowing there would be more later. "Thank you for rescuing us." She'd never forget the look of terror in his eyes when she'd opened her apartment door. "Not many people would have risked their lives like that."

"I couldn't have lived with myself if I hadn't. I care for all three of you." He brushed the hair away from her face. "Very much." The intensity of his gaze said so much more than his words. But now wasn't the time to explore that.

"Let's go to the farmhouse."

Chapter Sixteen

Rae woke just past eight thirty the next morning and quietly slipped out of the bedroom, not wanting to wake Maggie and Max. With all the stress of last night, she couldn't turn them down when they'd asked to sleep with her. She rubbed a hand over her face, trying to remember the last time she'd slept this late. Not that she'd done much sleeping.

They'd arrived at the farmhouse somewhere after two, reeking of smoke, so she and the kids rinsed off in the shower. Since they'd had no fresh clothes to put on, Cole had given the kids a couple of oversize T-shirts and found a fuzzy pink zip-up robe that'd belonged to his mother for Rae. Then she tossed their pajamas into the washer, so they'd at least have something clean to put on this morning. Of course, she'd have to put them in the dryer first.

She padded across the worn wooden floor in the hall, through the living room and into the kitchen, the aroma of coffee growing stronger with each step. When she entered the kitchen, she was surprised to find a fresh pot of coffee beside the sink and a box of doughnuts on the counter with a note attached.

Merry Christmas Eve! What better way to celebrate than with festive doughnuts? The kids will love them. Creamer is in the refrigerator for you. Of course, you can have a doughnut, too, if you like. There're plenty.

Wes and I are meeting at the café to make sure everything is secure. I'll be by once we're finished. Oh, and your clothes are in the dryer.
Cole

Her heart flip-flopped when she lifted the lid on the box to see chocolate and glazed doughnuts with red-and-green sprinkles on top. Was her favorite attorney actually getting into the holiday spirit? Or was this gesture simply because he knew how much it would mean to her? Whatever the case, it only made her love him all the more.

I care for all three of you.

That was such a lawyerly sort of statement. One she could easily discount or read too much into, so she'd best not dwell on it at all.

After pouring herself a cup of coffee, she changed into her red-and-green-plaid flannel pajama bottoms and green T-shirt before tugging on the yellow socks with grippers Johanna had given her while they were in the ambulance. Not the best outfit for shopping, but she and the kids needed clothes and shoes, so she had no choice.

She'd just settled into one of the wood chairs at the table with her coffee and a chocolate doughnut when she heard titters coming from the hall. The sound warmed her heart and gave her hope that perhaps last night's events wouldn't leave Maggie and Max permanently scarred.

Taking a bite, she said, "These sure are good doughnuts. I hope I don't eat them all before Maggie and Max wake up."

The pitter-patter of little feet grew louder until they appeared in the doorway.

"We have doughnuts?" Max's eyes actually sparkled.

"Mr. Cole got them for us." She gestured to the box that now sat on the table. "And guess what?"

"What?" Maggie hopped up on the chair.

"They're *Christmas* doughnuts." Rae lifted the lid to cheers from both kids.

Max had just taken his first bite when he met Rae's gaze across the table. "Are we going to get a Christmas tree for this house?"

Rae's heart ached. "Probably not, Max. Today is Christmas Eve, so I doubt there will be any Christmas trees left."

"But then it can't be Christmas," he said.

Rae simply stared at the boy. Had her emphasis on decorations and traditions led the boy to believe that was what Christmas was all about? Yes, she'd had nativities in both her apartment and the café, but they weren't big and showy like the Christmas trees she'd put up. Had she neglected to tell these two precious children the true meaning of Christmas?

"Max, Christmas isn't—"

A knock at the front door interrupted her. "I wonder who that is." Cole would've come through the back. She pushed out of her chair and moved through the living room to the small entry hall, Maggie and Max at her heels. After twisting the dead bolt, she pulled the door open.

"Merry Christmas!" Paisley, Christa, Laurel and all of their children stood on the front porch, wearing big smiles, their arms full of bags and boxes.

"What are y'all doing here? How did you—?"

"This is Bliss, remember?" Christa pulled the screen door open. "Where news travels faster than the speed of light."

Rae watched, dumbfounded, as they poured into the house, rapidly filling the living room.

"We brought groceries, clothes, toiletries," said Paisley. "And, of course, Christmas cookies."

"I pickeded out this outfit for you, Maggie." Sadie tugged a frilly red-and-white, two-piece set from a bag.

"And don't forget the Christmas tree," said Paisley's stepson, David.

Max's face lit up.

Tears pricked the backs of Rae's eyes. "You guys…" She sniffed. "Y'all are the best."

Her sister-in-law moved beside her, and Rae reached for baby Wyatt. "Cole called Wes first thing this morning. They're boarding up the café now."

Rae snuggled her nephew closer, savoring his baby scent. "I don't suppose he told you he saved our lives, did he?"

Laurel's eyes went wide. "Really?"

Nodding, Rae said, "If he hadn't banged down our door, we probably wouldn't be standing here now."

After Rae and the kids changed into real clothes, courtesy of her friends, Christa, Paisley and all of the kids except for Wyatt set to work in the living room, decorating a faux seven-foot blue spruce with colored lights, while Laurel and Rae put away groceries. Wes soon joined them.

"Where's Cole?" Rae stacked some canned goods in the cupboard, trying not to sound too disappointed.

"He said he had some errands to run."

The doorbell rang and Rae scurried through the living room, enjoying the sounds of happy children and Christmas music.

She yanked the door open to find Irma Corwin, one of the elderly ladies from church, standing there holding a foil-covered pan.

"Merry Christmas, Rae." The silver-haired woman's smile abruptly morphed into a frown. "I supposed you're not feeling too merry right about now, but speaking as someone who was forced out of her home due to circumstances beyond my control, I have no doubt you will bounce back from this tragedy. Least, that's what I'm praying for."

Rae couldn't help smiling. An undetected water leak had caused Irma's upstairs bathtub to come crashing into her downstairs family room almost two years ago. "Irma, it's those prayers that I know are going to get me through this." She pushed open the screen door. "Come on in and say hi to everyone."

"Don't mind if I do." The octogenarian carefully stepped inside. "I brought you some homemade macaroni and cheese, because I know how much those little ones love their mac and cheese."

"They are going to love that, Irma. Thank you." Rae started to close the door.

"Wait!"

Pulling it back open, Rae peered outside and saw Susan Salinas topping the steps, holding three wrapped gifts in one hand and a plastic grocery bag in the other.

"Susan, you didn't have to—"

"None of us ever has to, Rae." She whisked past her and continued into the house. "We just want to. I mean, you and the café are at the heart of Bliss."

Rae's heart swelled. "You have no idea how much that means to me."

"Now, before you go and make me cry, I know this may sound silly, but I brought you condiments." The mayor gestured to the bag. "Ketchup, mustard, mayo, ranch dressing, peanut butter, jelly. All those things we take for granted and never realize we don't have until we need them."

"Susan, you are a genius. I never would have thought of that, but you're so right."

"Oh—" she held out the pretty wrapped packages then "—and these are for you and the kids."

Now Rae was really going to get weepy. "Aww, you brought me a gift?"

"Hey, even big girls like their presents."

Rae hugged her then. "I can't tell you how much this means to me."

The same scenes continued throughout the morning and early afternoon—townsfolk dropping off clothing, shoes, food and anything else they thought she and the kids might need. Rae had never been on the receiving end of such an outpouring of love, and their generosity overwhelmed her. She couldn't think of a single thing she lacked.

Except maybe one very dapper attorney. And by the time her friends and her brother left to tend to their own Christmas plans, she couldn't help wondering where Cole was. She knew he'd been a driving force behind much of what had transpired today, so why wasn't he there? Then again, he hadn't done anything that would indicate he'd changed his mind about not spending Christmas with her and the kids.

Sorrow gripped her as she emptied another

bag of groceries, until a knock pulled her from her thoughts.

"Rae?"

She looked up to see Cole standing at the back door.

"Can we come in?"

"We?"

"Gary's with me."

"Absolutely." She stopped what she was doing and wiped her hands on a paper towel as the kids raced toward Cole.

"Mr. Cole, people brought us presents and food and a Christmas tree," said Max.

"It was like a big party," added Maggie.

"I'm sorry I missed it." He stepped aside as the fire chief entered.

Gary let out a low whistle. "It appears the people of Bliss really love you, Rae."

"Trust me, I am feeling the love." If only she'd feel it from Cole. "This has been one incredible day."

"Before I head on home and start celebrating with my family, I wanted to let you know that the cause of the fire appears to be faulty wiring on the refrigerator compressor."

She felt her jaw drop. "You're kidding. That's a brand-new compressor."

He lifted a shoulder. "Well, I guess you got a bad one then." He shoved his hands into the pockets of his jacket. "Oh, and I found something in the ashes I thought you might like to have." Stepping toward her, he reached out and handed her a small figurine.

She peered down at it, her heart filling with joy as her eyes filled with tears. "Maggie and Max, come here, please."

Despite their skeptical expressions, they complied.

Kneeling to their level, she held up the figurine. "Do you know Who this is?"

"It's the baby Jesus from the nativty."

She smiled at Max's pronunciation. "That's right." She sniffed. "Jesus is what Christmas is all about, not Christmas trees or presents or perfection. Christmas is about love. Like Jesus' sacrificial love."

"What does that mean?" Maggie cocked her little head.

"It means putting others first."

"Like when I let Max go down the slide first?"

"Something like that, yes." She paused. "Do you know who Jesus is?"

"God's son," they said together.

"Oh, you guys are so smart. Jesus is the son of God. He came to earth as a baby to teach us how to love so that we could have a life full of love and peace, even when things don't go the way we'd planned."

Looking up at Cole, she smiled. She'd never felt more loved. And seeing the grins on Max's and Maggie's faces, she knew that no matter what, this Christmas would be truly perfect.

Cole had never looked forward to Christmas the way he was anticipating this one. Everything about it felt different. Hopeful. Even the house he'd dreaded stepping into most of his life had a completely different feel. It could've had something to with the festive decorations or the merry music, but both of those things had been there in the past and never made him feel this way. He could only conclude that it was the people in the house who'd made the difference. The smiles, the laughter, the happiness they exuded.

Indeed, all of those things had played a role, but Cole knew the biggest change had been in him. By the grace of God, his joy had been restored, and that was the greatest gift Cole could have received. It had been decades since he'd dared to dream of a future, but now it was all he could think of, and he could hardly wait to share it with Rae.

They'd taken the kids to the Christmas Eve service at church earlier and were now preparing to enjoy some of the food people had dropped off throughout the day.

While Rae got things ready, he sat at the kitchen table with the kids, listening to them recount everything that had happened today. Not once did they mention the fire or anything from last night. Instead, they focused on all the good that had taken place as a result of being forced from their home. He watched them in amazement, knowing there was so much he could learn from them.

A knock at the back door had him looking across the kitchen to Rae. "Are you expecting someone?"

She continued to work. "Maybe it's someone with more food. Would you mind getting it for me?"

Standing, he moved to the door and pulled it open, surprised to see Mick on the other side of the screen door, holding a Christmassy box with a bow on top. "What brings you out tonight?" Cole would've thought he'd be with his family.

Mick smiled and pulled the screen door open wide enough to pass the lidded box to Cole. "Special delivery."

Looking from the box to his friend, he hesitated a moment before taking hold. Perhaps it was something for the kids. Rae had probably known about it, but had forgotten in all the chaos of the last twenty-four hours.

"Thanks."

Mick waved. "Y'all have a merry Christmas."

Cole closed the door as their friend descended the back steps then turned to Rae. "I'm assuming this is for you."

Without looking up, she continued to arrange cookies on a plate. "Does it have a tag?"

He glanced at the package. "Why does it have my name on it?"

"What is it?" Maggie hurried to his side with her brother in tow.

Only then did Cole hear a hint of a whimper through some holes in the side of the box. His heart all but stopped as his suddenly watery gaze sought out Rae's. "For me?"

Her smile was wide, adding a spark to her beautiful blue eyes. "Merry Christmas."

He hurriedly set the box on the table and lifted the lid to discover a golden retriever puppy with a big red bow around its neck nestled inside. He scooped it out and held it close, breathing in that sweet puppy smell as Maggie and Max cooed over it.

"It's so cute!" Maggie scratched its head.

"What's its name?" Max petted it, too.

"We'll have to leave that up to Mr. Cole." Rae wiped her hands and moved toward them.

"He sure is a cute little fella." She rubbed behind its ears.

"It's a boy?" Cole couldn't seem to stop smiling. Strange that he'd never considered having a dog before when it seemed like the most natural thing in the world.

She nodded.

"What are you going to name him, Mr. Cole?" Maggie peered up at him.

He stroked the little fur ball under the chin. "Well, I'm kind of partial to the name Bo." He looked at Rae. "What do you think?"

"I think it's perfect."

Later, after their bellies were full of some of the best food Bliss had to offer, they took Bo outside to take care of business before the kids donned their Christmas pajamas and settled on the couch with him and Rae for the reading of the Christmas story.

When Rae asked Cole to read, he was hesitant. And then he remembered the way she'd talked to the kids earlier in the day, explaining to them what Christmas was all about. Even as he read the story that he'd heard so many times throughout his life, he found himself seeing things in a different light. Instead of viewing it as a tale that had been passed down through generations, he was able to focus on the gift that had been given to the world in the form of a baby. A child who would one day lay down his life for mankind.

Jesus knew the pain of abuse and rejection. Yet He chose to love anyway.

Once the kids were in bed—which took a lot longer than usual with the anticipation of Christmas and the addition of a puppy—Cole joined Rae at the kitchen table to help her wrap some of the gifts people had brought. He couldn't believe someone had even brought wrapping paper, bows, scissors and tape.

Adding a bow to the box he'd just wrapped, he said, "Max is going to be one happy camper with all of this dinosaur stuff." Coloring books, action figures, even some that made sounds.

"Yeah." Rae cut another swath of paper, her single word coming out almost as a sigh. "I'm afraid Maggie is going to be disappointed, though."

Only then did he remember he still had stuff in the back of his truck. "Not on my watch, she won't."

"What?"

Setting Max's gift aside, he stood. "Keep an eye on Bo for me. I'll be right back." He hurried into the cool night air to retrieve a large box from the back seat of his truck.

When he returned to the kitchen, he set it on the table. "Remember I bought a second doll along with a bunch of other games and toys for the silent auction?"

"Yes." Her pretty brow arched.

"I remembered Clare Kingston had won it, so I paid her a visit today to see if I could buy that second doll for Maggie."

Rae's eyes widened with hope. "And?"

"She wasn't willing to sell it."

Rae's shoulders slumped.

"However, she was more than happy to *give* it to me, along with anything else in the basket I thought Maggie and Max might like."

"Seriously?" Rae's expression brightened. "There's an—" she glanced toward the opening to the living room, then lowered her voice "—Emma Country Girl doll in there?"

He nodded, savoring the look of sheer delight on her face. "Along with a couple of games and some trinkets."

"So that's why you were gone so long." She hopped up from her chair and rounded the table to give him a hug. "I can't believe you did that." Releasing him, she stared into his eyes, her palms resting against his chest. "That's not true, actually. I *can* believe you did it. What I can't believe is that you didn't tell me."

Looping his arms around her waist to prevent her from escaping, he said, "A guy's gotta have a few surprises."

"I see." Her expression turned coy. "Do you have any other surprises you'd like to share?"

"As a matter of fact, there is one." He tugged her closer, unable to stop smiling. "I love you, Rae."

She stared up at him, blinking. "You do?"

"More than words can say. I'm just sorry it took me so long to realize it. But when I saw that fire last night, the only thing I could think of was that if something happened, I'd never get to tell you how I felt."

Her gaze never left his. "I'm so thankful you saved us because now I get to tell you that I love you, too."

Unable to wait any longer, he lowered his head and claimed her sweet lips, this time without regret or fear but with a desire to walk through life alongside her and make every one of her dreams come true.

When they parted, he rested his forehead against hers. "This might be a little too soon to say this, but I want us to be a family. I want to be a husband to you and a father to Maggie and Max." He released her then, reached into his pocket and pulled out a velvet box, praying he wasn't about to completely mess things up. "I guess what I'm trying to say is—" he lifted the lid on the box to reveal a brilliant cushion-cut diamond ring "—will you marry me, Rae?"

Her stunned gaze moved from his face to the ring and back again several times. "I... I can't—"

His body tightened. She was going to say no. It was too soon.

Finally, she looked him in the eye, holding his attention. "I can't believe this is happening. Yes, yes, a thousand times yes. I will marry you, Cole Heinsohn." She threw her arms around his neck, pushed up on her toes and kissed him with an intensity that left no room for doubt.

Cole knew this was going to be a Christmas he would never forget. And, Lord willing, there would be many more to come.

Epilogue

❧

One year later

Two days before Christmas, Rae danced around the new and much improved kitchen at the farmhouse with a baby on her hip as Burl Ives encouraged her to have a *holly jolly Christmas*. Laurel, Christa and Paisley would be there soon with their families for an early Christmas gathering.

Now that they all had kids, they were busier than ever, leaving them less and less time to come together. She still couldn't get over how much their lives had changed in the last few years, each of them going from contentedly single to married with families.

She and Cole had exchanged vows in February, only weeks before the reopening of the café. Then, as soon as the renovations were completed there, they'd put Wes to work updating the farmhouse, giving them a welcoming space for their growing family.

Maggie and Max officially became Heinsohns in June. A few weeks later, six-week-old Amelia came to them via the foster system, setting Rae and Cole on an entirely different journey with an infant.

She kissed the top of the now six-month-old's downy head. Barring anything unforeseen, the child would be theirs forever in a few short weeks.

As the pitter-patter of children's feet echoed over her head, along with the tit-tat of Bo's claws as he followed them around, Rae paused to savor the moment. Chaotic as it often was, this was exactly the kind of life Rae had always wanted. Though it may not have been in her timing or in a traditional manner, her dream of becoming a mother had finally come true. And the best part was getting to experience it alongside Cole. He was her partner in every way and had wasted no time settling into the role of father. Whether he was playing with the older kids or cuddling little Amelia, her heart nearly burst every time she saw him loving on them. She couldn't imagine life without him.

"They're here! They're here!" Maggie and

Max cheered as they hurried down the steps, Bo barking behind them.

Rae passed through the living room to meet them, smiling at her husband who trailed the trio.

"Their rooms are finally clean." He reached for Amelia, kissing her cheek before cradling her in his arms. "You're not going to make any messes, are you, sweetness?" He tickled the babe under the chin, making her grin. "You can be my little neat freak."

Rae released a sigh. "Ah, if only."

She fell in behind the two older kids and opened the door as Sarah-Jane bounded onto the porch. Behind her, Laurel held Wyatt's hand as he toddled toward the steps, while Wes toted the carrier containing the latest addition to their family, Hannah-Grace, who'd arrived in early October.

"Here comes Sadie." Maggie pointed to the drive as Mick's pickup pulled in. Paisley's SUV was right behind him.

Soon the house was filled with their friends, along with the sights, sounds and smells of the season, bringing back all those cherished memories from Rae's childhood.

With greetings exchanged and presents tucked under the tree, the men took the kids out back to play while the four women who'd come to Bliss in search of fresh starts gathered in the kitchen with the babies and the food.

"It doesn't seem that long ago it was just the four of us." Paisley drizzled a balsamic glaze over the freshly roasted brussels sprouts.

"I remember our first Christmas together." Laurel removed a whimpering Hannah-Grace from her seat. "I was pregnant with Sarah-Jane."

"Can y'all believe that was four years ago?" Christa held Amelia, swaying back and forth.

"Who would've thought we'd *all* end up married with kids?" Rae pulled the ham from the oven.

Christa shook her head. "Definitely not me."

"Me, either." Rae eyed her friends over her shoulder. "At least, not the married part."

"If I'm counting correctly," said Laurel, "our numbers have gone from just the four of us to *seventeen*."

Paisley grinned. "God is pretty fantastic, isn't He?"

"He certainly is." Rae's gaze drifted to little Amelia. "He brought some really amazing guys into our lives and gave us the children our hearts longed for."

"Just goes to show that nothing is too big for God," said Christa.

"Amen," the other three women said collectively.

The back door flew open then and the kids burst into the house, Maggie in the lead.

"What's going on?" Rae watched as they rushed past.

Max stopped and peered up at her with those dark eyes. "Maggie's going to play piano so we can all sing Christmas carols."

"Come sing with us." Sadie motioned as she went by.

As everyone gathered in the living room for a round of "Jingle Bells," Cole whisked Rae out onto the back porch.

He slipped an arm around her waist and pulled her against him. "Is this the kind of Christmas you enjoyed as a kid?"

"Let's see." She eyed the freshly painted beadboard ceiling. "Decorations? Check. Cookies? Check. Gingerbread houses? Check."

"And everyone is singing in our living room like the final scene in *It's a Wonderful Life.*"

"In that case—" she wound her arms around his neck "—this is even better than those Christmases I remember."

"Because everyone is singing?"

"No, because I get to share all of it with you and the kids. Yes, I love the traditions and tend to get caught up in all the hype, but even if we had nothing, as long as we were together, it would be the best Christmas ever."

His hold on her tightened. "Thank you for showing me how full life can be."

"You're welcome. Now kiss me before someone realizes we're missing and comes searching for us."

Wearing a mischievous smile, he lowered his head. As Cole's lips touched hers, Rae thanked God for His many blessings. Yes, she'd known loss that had threatened to cripple her, but through it all she'd chosen to trust God, knowing He would never forsake her. And with Cole by her side, they were free to enjoy the abundant life God had planned specifically for them.

And that was the greatest gift she'd ever received.

* * * * *

Dear Reader,

Some characters are difficult to say goodbye to, and Rae, Paisley, Christa and Laurel definitely fall into that category. But knowing they're living the lives God had planned specifically for them certainly makes it easier.

I don't know about you, but when it comes to Christmas, I tend to be a lot like Rae. The decorations, the foods, the traditions…it's easy for me to get so caught up in everything that I forget to focus on the true meaning of Christmas—a baby born to save the world. Jesus is the greatest gift any of us could receive.

The thing about a gift, though, is that it's not just about receiving but accepting. When life is filled with hardships the way Cole's was, accepting can be a challenge. When so little is in our control, we tend to cling to what we know. But we don't have to be a slave to those hardships because Jesus experienced them, too. He suffered rejection, abuse, hunger, betrayal, loss, and so much more. Yet because of His great love for us, He left the glory of Heaven to walk this earth and gave His life so that we could spend eternity with Him. All He asks us to do is to accept His gift of salvation.

I hope you enjoyed this final visit to Bliss, Texas, though I have a feeling it won't be forgotten. Only time will tell. Until then, I would love to hear from you. You can contact me via my website, mindyobenhaus.com, or you can snail-mail me c/o Love Inspired Books, 195 Broadway, 24th Floor, New York, NY 10007.

May the joy of Christmas fill your heart throughout the year,

Mindy

Get 4 **FREE REWARDS!**

We'll send you 2 FREE Books plus 2 FREE Mystery Gifts.

Love Inspired books feature uplifting stories where faith helps guide you through life's challenges and discover the promise of a new beginning.

FREE Value Over **$20**

Get 4 FREE REWARDS!

We'll send you 2 FREE Books plus 2 FREE Mystery Gifts.

Harlequin Heartwarming Larger-Print books will connect you to uplifting stories where the bonds of friendship, family and community unite.

FREE
Value Over
$20

YES! Please send me 2 FREE Harlequin Heartwarming Larger-Print novels and my 2 FREE mystery gifts (gifts worth about $10 retail). After receiving them, if I don't wish to receive any more books, I can return the shipping statement marked "cancel." If I don't cancel, I will receive 4 brand-new larger-print novels every month and be billed just $5.74 per book in the U.S. or $6.24 per book in Canada. That's a savings of at least 21% off the cover price. It's quite a bargain! Shipping and handling is just 50¢ per book in the U.S. and $1.25 per book in Canada.* I understand that accepting the 2 free books and gifts places me under no obligation to buy anything. I can always return a shipment and cancel at any time. The free books and gifts are mine to keep no matter what I decide.

161/361 HDN GNPZ

Name (please print)

Address   Apt. #

City   State/Province   Zip/Postal Code

Email: Please check this box ☐ if you would like to receive newsletters and promotional emails from Harlequin Enterprises ULC and its affiliates. You can unsubscribe anytime.

Mail to the **Harlequin Reader Service:**
IN U.S.A.: P.O. Box 1341, Buffalo, NY 14240-8531
IN CANADA: P.O. Box 603, Fort Erie, Ontario L2A 5X3

Want to try 2 free books from another series? Call 1-800-873-8635 or visit www.ReaderService.com.

---

*Terms and prices subject to change without notice. Prices do not include sales taxes, which will be charged (if applicable) based on your state or country of residence. Canadian residents will be charged applicable taxes. Offer not valid in Quebec. This offer is limited to one order per household. Books received may not be as shown. Not valid for current subscribers to Harlequin Heartwarming Larger-Print books. All orders subject to approval. Credit or debit balances in a customer's account(s) may be offset by any other outstanding balance owed by or to the customer. Please allow 4 to 6 weeks for delivery. Offer available while quantities last.

Your Privacy—Your information is being collected by Harlequin Enterprises ULC, operating as Harlequin Reader Service. For a complete summary of the information we collect, how we use this information and to whom it is disclosed, please visit our privacy notice located at corporate.harlequin.com/privacy-notice. From time to time we may also exchange your personal information with reputable third parties. If you wish to opt out of this sharing of your personal information, please visit readerservice.com/consumerschoice or call 1-800-873-8635. **Notice to California Residents**—Under California law, you have specific rights to control and access your data. For more information on these rights and how to exercise them, visit corporate.harlequin.com/california-privacy. HW21R2